Before she could say a word he brushed his thumb over her lips, but this time the action was slower, more sensual, more intense.

There was no excuse of milk froth being on her lip—just pure desire. It was as though he wanted to touch her, to excite her, to let her see herself through his eyes, and the fact that he'd caressed her facial scars and wasn't presently running for the hills was a good beginning. But could she trust him?

Jane pushed the thought away, intent on focusing on the here and now as Sean's thumb tenderly traced her lower lip, causing her to draw in her breath. Her entire body was flooded with tingles and anticipatory delight.

'I wish you wouldn't—' She stopped, unable to speak, unable to concentrate, unable to do anything but feel. Her eyelids fluttered closed. 'You... We shouldn't...' she whispered, her words barely audible.

'Why shouldn't we?'

Sean's words were husky, and when she risked opening her eyes to look into his she was stunned to find him looking at her with intense desire. No. That couldn't be right.

For so long—for too many years—she'd always believed bad things about herself. She'd been told all her life that she was nothing special, and now, seeing Sean looking at her like that, telling her he didn't think she was ugly...was it possible for her to believe him?

'Jane...'

He breathed her name and before she knew what was happening he'd bent his head and brushed a light, feathery kiss across her cheek. 'You clearly have no idea just how much you've infiltrated my thoughts.'

Dear Reader

While I was writing HIS DIAMOND LIKE NO OTHER it was winter in Australia. The cold, the rain and catching the inevitable cold. I was lying in my bed, sneezing and snuffling and generally feeling sorry for myself, but thankfully I had Jane and Sean to brighten my day and keep me company. This also might explain why HIS DIAMOND LIKE NO OTHER is set in summer! Oh, I could just *feel* that glorious sun on my face as I entered their lives.

HIS DIAMOND LIKE NO OTHER is also my 60th Mills & Boon® Medical Romance™ title. I confess at times it was very difficult to write, because I wanted to make it extra-special, extra-memorable and extra-gut-wrenchingly heartfelt. I do love Jane—so very much—but the thing I love most is that even though she's experienced some emotionally distressing times she hasn't let it beat her. She's been forced to save herself, to become a strong, independent woman, and it's these very qualities that attract Sean to her.

Sean made me smile and laugh and clap my hands like a silly schoolgirl. He has such presence and drive, and a loving, supportive family. I delighted at his relationship with his son, as well as the closeness he shares with his parents and sisters. Family is important, and Sean is not only able to show Jane that, but to open up his world and share it with her. Now, *that's* being a true hero!

I hope you enjoy HIS DIAMOND LIKE NO OTHER.

Warmest regards

Lucy

HIS DIAMOND
LIKE NO OTHER

BY
LUCY CLARK

Published in Great Britain 2014
by Mills & Boon, an imprint of Harlequin (UK) Limited,
Eton House, 18-24 Paradise Road, Richmond, Surrey, TW9 1SR

© 2014 Anne Clark & Peter Clark

ISBN: 978 0 263 24373 4

Lucy Clark is actually a husband-and-wife writing team. They enjoy taking holidays with their children, during which they discuss and develop new ideas for their books using the fantastic Australian scenery. They use their daily walks to talk over characterisation and fine details of the wonderful stories they produce, and are avid movie buffs. They live on the edge of a popular wine district in South Australia with their two children, and enjoy spending family time together at weekends.

Recent titles by Lucy Clark:

These books are also available in eBook format from www.millsandboon.co.uk

DEDICATION

To Mum & Dad.

Even though I'm all grown up now, I still need you both.
Thank you for always being supportive and generous and loving.
—Ps 103

HIS DIAMOND LIKE NO OTHER
is Lucy Clark's 60th book for Mills & Boon®!

Praise for
Lucy Clark:

'A sweet and fun romance about second chances
and second love.'
—*HarlequinJunkie.com* on
DARE SHE DREAM OF FOREVER?

CHAPTER ONE

'So. It *is* you.'

Sean Booke's deep voice vibrated through Jane's body, causing her insides to tremble. She closed her eyes for a split second and forced herself to remain calm, at least on the outside. It wouldn't do to allow her ex-brother-in-law to rile her. Pasting on a polite smile, she turned to look at him, unconsciously shifting her glasses and straightening her shoulders, tugging at the sleeves of her top to ensure they covered her wrists. It was a defence mechanism, developed over many years to hide the scars which were a permanent reminder of the darkest time in her life.

Sean Booke stood before her, more vibrant, more handsome, more intimidating than he'd been the last time she'd seen him, which had been three years ago at her sister's funeral. Back then he'd been dressed in a black suit, which had perfectly matched his mood, and at the wake she'd had little chance to speak to him as he'd somehow managed to manoeuvre his way around to the opposite side of the room to wherever she'd been.

Eventually she'd received the message. Sean hadn't wanted to speak to her and it appeared, given the gruffness of his tone, that nothing had changed. He carried a small, slim computer tablet as well as two sets of patient files. Jane cleared her throat.

'How are you, Sean?' She silently congratulated herself on her polite, impersonal tone as she headed into the paediatric ward conference room ahead of him, wishing she hadn't been adamant about being early for her first scheduled ward round. She was nervous enough, not only about starting her new job but about Sean's reaction to her presence at his hospital.

He ignored her question, his brow deeply furrowed as he followed her. '*You're* the new paediatrician?'

'Correct.'

She turned and looked at him, pleased they were alone for this conversation. It had been inevitable, especially when she'd accepted the position at Adelaide's Children's Hospital. There was no coincidence about it. She'd decided it was time for her to return to Adelaide, to work at this particular hospital, the hospital where, at the age of thirteen, she'd been a patient. It was time she made the effort to put her ghosts to rest but she had to admit that Sean Booke was far from a ghost, especially with the way his spicy scent seemed to wind itself around her.

'I couldn't believe it when I read the inter-office memo announcing your arrival. Specialist paediatrician in juvenile eating disorders.' He put his bundle of notes and computer tablet onto the table then stared at her, as though he really could not believe it. Jane tried not to tug on her baggy top, which hung rather low over her ankle-length skirt. Fashion had never been her thing; instead, she'd focused on studying and getting good grades.

'I mean, how many Jane Diamonds are there in the world?' Sean shook his head, his words still filled with an angry bitterness that was simmering just below the surface. He turned and walked over to the window. 'How long is your contract?'

'Twelve months.' She wanted to tell him she hadn't

meant to cause him any pain but she didn't think he'd believe her. As far as Sean was concerned, he'd tarred her
with the same brush as Daina. The fact that Jane had always been the polar opposite of her older sister clearly was
of little concern to him.

'And you *chose* to come here? You knew this was *my*
hospital.'

'I was *invited* to come and work here, Sean. I just didn't
turn it down.'

'You?' He glanced at her over his shoulder, frown still
in place. 'You were head-hunted? By whom?'

'Luc Bourgeois.' Jane tried to be brave, tried to hold his
piercing blue gaze. She pushed her glasses onto her nose
and nodded. 'I guess my past experience working with
Professor Edna Robe has finally paid off.'

'Robe? World-leading specialist in the field of paediatric eating disorders?'

Jane raised her chin, telling herself she had no reason
to hide her successes. 'I've co-authored five papers with
her and presented our findings two months ago at an eating disorder conference in Argentina.'

He turned from the window, arms still crossed, and
looked at her more closely. 'Huh!' was all he said, leaving
Jane to ponder what on earth that might mean.

They remained silent for a minute, Jane wondering
whether she should say something else, anything else,
rather than stand here and not speak a word. Sean was the
man who had been married to her sister, he was the father
of her only living blood relative—six-year-old Spencer.
She was desperate to ask him about her nephew but wasn't
sure, given the reception she'd just received, whether that
was a good idea. Then again, perhaps he might think her
strange if she *didn't* ask.

'You need more confidence in yourself, Jane,' Professor Robe had said to her late last year, hence why Jane had been the one presenting the paper in Argentina. Confidence? She had confidence in spades when it came to treating and caring for her young patients but a one-on-one confrontation with the man who had the power to refuse her request was bringing her inner doubts to the fore. She had to get past it.

'How's Spencer?' The words were out of her mouth before she could stop and analyse them any further.

Sean's frown returned but it wasn't as deep as it had previously been. 'He's fine.'

'How's he doing in school?' Now that she'd opened the discussion, she really did want to know more. She had so many questions about her nephew, along with the wish that Sean would grant her access to him.

'Fine.'

'Does he have any plans for his birthday? A present list? I'd rather get him something he really wants than have to guess.' Good heavens. She was starting to babble now.

The arms tightened defensively over his chest and Jane found herself momentarily distracted by the way his crisp white shirt pulled around his biceps. She tried to school her senses. Of course Sean was a dynamic, good-looking man. It was the reason her wayward sister had been attracted to him in the first place.

'Why do you want to know about Spencer? You've never shown more than a passing interest in him before now.'

Jane felt as though he'd slapped her as that clearly wasn't true. 'I've sent Christmas and birthday presents every year,' she defended, feeling her temper beginning to rise. Usually, she was quite a calm and controlled woman but when she thought about facing her future, one of only work and loneliness, she was filled with desperation...

desperation to make sure that *didn't* happen. Now she was desperate to make sure Sean realised just how much she loved her nephew, even though she didn't know him as well as she would have liked.

'And you've always been more than generous with your gifts. Still, you've never made any effort to see him.'

'Any effor—' She broke off her incredulous reply as two paediatric nurses walked into the conference room, greeting Sean with bright smiles. Jane boxed up her simmering anger at Sean and put it aside, pulling on her professionalism. When Sean made no effort to introduce Jane, instead immersing himself in setting up his computer and connecting it to the equipment in the room, Jane forced herself to step forward and hold out her hand. 'Hi. I'm Jane Diamond.'

'Oh the new paediatrician, the eating disorder specialist,' one of the women stated, shaking Jane's hand. 'Welcome. I'm Anthea. This is Romana. We're really glad you're here. Such a necessary sub-speciality you cover.' Anthea was still nodding as she spoke. 'Let us know if you need help settling in or finding your way about the hospital.'

Jane smiled, ignoring Sean's presence completely. 'I was actually a patient here, in this very ward, when I was thirteen.'

'Really?'

'Wow.'

'It doesn't seem like the general hospital layout has changed all that much since then.'

'Sad but true,' Romana said with a laugh.

'At least the equipment's been updated,' Anthea added, smiling. As more people came into the conference room, Anthea made sure Jane was introduced. Sean had moved to the corner of the room and she could almost feel him watching her, but every time she glanced in his direction he was either deeply engrossed in conversation with someone else or looking at a set of scans that were due to be discussed during the short prelude before the ward round.

The pre-ward round began with head of unit, Luc Bourgeois, introducing her. 'Jane and I worked together in Paris for twelve months and I have to say, when she finally agreed to my constant pleading to come and work here, I was relieved. Eating disorders, especially amongst children under the age of eight, have gone unchecked for too long. This hospital plans to change that. Jane will be undertaking a research project whilst she's here and I'm expecting everyone to afford her every professional courtesy with regard to patient care and participating with the project if required.'

'Absolutely,' Anthea agreed, and a few people even gave Jane a smattering round of applause. She felt highly self-conscious standing in front of everyone but forced herself to smile and nod. Standing in front of a lecture room full of people wasn't her favourite thing to do but she was forcing herself to get used to it. What made today's experience even more unnerving was the fact that she was so highly aware of Sean's presence.

He was standing at the front of the room as well, waiting to present an interesting case for discussion before they all headed out to begin the ward round. When Luc had finished successfully embarrassing her by listing all her accomplishments, as well as sharing one or two small anecdotes of the time they'd worked together in Paris several years ago, Jane went to move to the side of the room but somehow managed to trip over her own feet and slam straight into Sean.

His hands immediately came around her waist, steadying her. Jane was minutely aware of the way his warmth seemed to surround her, of the way his firm muscled torso pressed against her shoulder, of the way his scent danced about her senses, creating a heady combination and one she was far from immune to.

A few of the people in the room chuckled, not unkindly, and Jane quickly collected herself, shifting awkwardly, wanting to put distance between them, but instead she ended up staring directly into Sean's eyes. Everything in the room seemed to freeze. She could hear the flutter of her eyelashes as she blinked once, then twice, the pounding of her heart against her chest and the way his breath seemed to mingle with hers.

'Steady on.' His deep voice was filled with concern, or so it seemed, but that couldn't be right. Sean didn't like her. Sean had never liked her. During the course of his marriage to her sister, they'd rarely spoken.

'Er...sorry,' Jane muttered, the world around her returning to normal speed. It felt as though she'd been pressed up against Sean's warm body for quite some time, although only a few seconds had passed. She jerked from his hands and he dropped them instantly, mildly surprised, as though he hadn't even realised he'd been touching her.

'And now Sean's going to present us with a few case studies, which I'd like everyone to pay close attention to during the ward round,' Luc announced, as Jane shifted towards the rear of the room, leaning against the wall, desperate to hide herself away in an attempt to recover her equilibrium.

She watched as Sean stepped forward to talk, using a small remote to produce a radiographic image on the audio-visual screen that was linked to his computer tablet. How could she have tripped like that? Fallen against *him*? She tried to swallow over her dry throat, surprised to find she was actually trembling from the encounter with him. He was *Sean*, for goodness' sake, and he didn't like her.

She breathed in, needing to gain some level of control over her senses, needing to concentrate on what Sean was saying, but all she was conscious of when she breathed in was the lingering spicy scent she'd always equated with him. It was the same cologne he'd worn all those years ago when they'd first met. She'd been nothing more than a braces-wearing student of seventeen, studying furiously for her final school exams, when Sean had married her sister.

The two had met in the emergency department at a hospital in Sydney. Daina had been holidaying with friends, partying too hard, and had badly twisted her ankle. Sean had been the intern who had treated her. Daina had left the hospital with a perfectly bandaged foot, a pair of crutches and a date.

After a whirlwind romance Daina had eventually told Jane that she wasn't coming back to live in Adelaide because she was married. Sean had accompanied his new wife back to Adelaide, met his new sister-in-law for the first time and casually suggested that with the subjects she was studying she could definitely get into medical school.

Even though Jane had been six months shy of her eighteenth birthday, Daina, who was her legal guardian, had upped and left, returning to Sydney with her new, handsome prize of a husband. Jane had seriously hoped that Sean would be able to fix Daina, that he'd realise she was suffering from some sort of multiple personality disorder, that he'd be able to get her the help she needed. But, almost six years later, after giving birth to a child she hadn't wanted, Daina had abandoned him and taken off. Three years after that, she was dead.

Jane was unable to believe the pain Daina had caused

her, not only after their parents' death but prior to it as well. In fact, it had been Daina who had caused the car accident that had robbed Jane of her parents at the age of thirteen. For years Jane had bottled up the resentment she'd felt towards her older sibling and she'd thought that coming home to Adelaide, making an effort to get to know Spencer as much as Sean would allow, she'd hopefully be able to put her past pain to rest.

'Jane? *Jane?*'

Her eyes snapped open to find Sean standing before her, the rest of the medical staff who had been attending the pre-ward round meeting filing out of the small conference room.

'Would you care to join us?' His tone was filled with derision but she watched his eyes widen slightly as she carefully lifted her glasses and dabbed at her eyes, annoyed with herself for not paying closer attention during the meeting and for tearing up in front of *him*.

'Are you all right?' His tone was still gruff but there was also a hint of confused concern.

Jane sniffed and settled her glasses on her nose. 'I'm fine.'

'You're not. I can hear it in your voice.'

'Leave it.' She went to step around him but he moved and blocked her way.

'You look like Daina when you do that. That "don't mess with me" look.'

Jane tilted her head and glared at him. 'Then remind me not to do it again.' She moved quickly, effectively sidestepping him, and followed the last of the staff out of the room.

It wasn't exactly the beginning she'd hoped for but, really, had she honestly expected Sean to accept her presence, especially when she clearly did remind him, in small ways, of his deceased wife?

* * *

'It's no use, Luc,' she told her friend a week later as they sat in the hospital cafeteria, enjoying a quick morning cuppa before the hecticness of their day descended. 'Sean has made it quite clear over the past week that he resents me being here.'

'Nonsense.' Luc dunked a piece of croissant in his coffee before eating it. 'He's just…getting used to the idea, that's all.'

Jane levelled him with a stare of disbelief and Luc had the audacity to laugh.

'It's true, Jane. When you first mentioned to me, all those years ago when we worked in Paris, that a man called Sean Booke was married to your sister, I thought nothing of it.'

'Because back then you had no idea who he was,' Jane pointed out.

'True, but then years later when I returned to Adelaide, who do I find myself working with? None other than your Sean Booke.' Luc finished off his croissant then spread his hands wide. 'It's one of the reasons why I encouraged you to come back to Adelaide, to get to know him. Sure, your sister has passed away but family is family. Plus, he's a nice guy, Jane.'

'To everyone but me.'

'So you admit he's good with the patients?'

Jane looked into her almost empty cup as she thought back to the way she'd watched Sean interact with the patients in the ward and she had to admit he was an excellent doctor. He wouldn't rush the kids if they had something to say; instead, he'd sit on their beds and listen patiently while they talked. In clinic, she had seen several of his patients coming out of his consulting room with wide, beaming smiles on their faces, their parents looking equally as pleased.

'Of course he's good with the patients,' she told Luc, 'otherwise you wouldn't have him working in your department.'

'Very true. I only employ the best—which is the other reason you're here because even without the prospect of getting to know your nephew, I still would have hounded you to work here. That was just my trump card.'

'I know.' Jane finished the rest of her drink, grimacing a little at the coolness of the liquid. 'We'd better go or we'll be late for the pre-ward round meeting.' They both stood and placed their cups on the dirty dishes rack before heading towards the ward. 'Will Sean be presenting another interesting case this week?'

'Yes. Why? Do you have an interesting case you'd like to share?'

'Not at this stage. I was just curious as to whether Sean always did the presenting or not.'

'He organises it so if you do have an interesting case, you'll need to speak to him.'

Jane filed that information away as they entered the room. This time, when Sean stood at the front of the staff at the meeting, discussing the noteworthy aspects of a newly admitted patient, Jane listened intently. She did her best to ignore the way his deep, smooth tones washed over her, and the way he gesticulated smoothly with his hands, pointing out the different methods of treatment that were projected onto the screen. He had lovely hands, she realised, gentle, caring hands, big and strong and able to support. The memory of him placing those hands at her waist the previous week, steadying her after she'd tripped, burst into her mind and it took all her willpower to dismiss it. She was here to concentrate on her patients, not on Sean Booke's hands!

During the following week Jane watched Sean help a ten-year-old boy come to a level of understanding with the diagnosis of leukaemia. She found him in the ward play-room, sitting on a chair that was way too small for him, colouring in with three other children, all of them laughing together. She also saw him agonising over the correct treatment plan for one of his older patients, a fifteen-year-old girl, Mya, whose lungs weren't responding to the usual asthma medications.

'How's Mya today?' Jane asked Sean a few days later. She'd entered the nurses' station to write up some case notes and within a matter of minutes, with nurses heading off to tend to their patients, she'd found herself alone with Sean at the desk. Having been at the hospital for two and a half weeks now, and having had several professional patient-related conversations with Sean without any mention of their shared personal connections, Jane felt more confident in enquiring about his patient. What she still found difficult to ignore was the subtle spicy scent surrounding him, one that definitely held appeal.

'Still not stabilising.' Sean shook his head slowly, before closing his eyes and pinching the bridge of his nose with his thumb and forefinger. 'I've tried everything. She responds to treatment for one, sometimes two days and then the symptoms return.'

'She's not reacting as expected to the corticosteroids? Has this happened before?'

Sean opened his eyes and handed Jane Mya's file. 'If you can find something I've missed, be my guest.' He slumped forward onto the desk, resting his head on his hands. He was tired, bewildered and very concerned about his patient. He'd consulted with the respiratory specialists yesterday afternoon but it was becoming clear that the corticosteroids might be doing more damage than good.

'Were you here all night?' Jane's words were quiet and when he lifted his head it was to find her watching him with professional empathy.

'Arrived around three this morning, as you would have seen in the notes.'

'But you didn't head over to the residential wing? Catch a few hours' extra sleep?'

Sean was too exhausted to try and look for any sort of ulterior motive for Jane's questions. 'I was worried about Mya. I did have a shower and change not too long ago, hoping to clear my mind a little and for the solution to miraculously present itself, but that hasn't happened.'

Jane smiled, a soft, delicate smile that softened her green eyes. Sean stared at her for a long moment, amazed at the difference in her features, especially the lack of that wariness in her gaze that had often been present whenever they'd been in the same room together. This morning she'd pulled her long, luscious locks back from her face into a simple ponytail, her fringe neatly combed over her forehead. She wore a long-sleeved cotton top, which hung low over an ankle-length black and white striped skirt. She was neat and tidy, calm and professional, and yet this morning there seemed to be something different about her, and it wasn't just the soft smile she was giving him.

She nodded. 'Sometimes it is impossible to sleep, especially when there's a patient puzzle to solve.'

Sean couldn't believe the way her calm, peaceful tone seemed to wash over him, alleviating some of the stress that had built up in his trapezius. He forced himself to look away from her, not wanting to be drawn in by Jane Diamond and her pretty smiles. While it was true that he'd been impressed with the way she'd settled into hospital life over the past weeks, relating to staff and patients in an easy, professional manner, she also represented a connection to his past and it was a past he'd locked securely away and didn't really fancy revisiting.

'And with your puzzle, I'd like to offer a suggestion, if I may,' she continued, watching as he angled his neck from side to side, trying to work out some of the kinks in his muscles. She had to resist the urge to stand behind him and gently massage his shoulders, as she would naturally offer to do for any of her other colleagues. Sean was different and with him it was imperative she keep her professional distance.

'What's that?' he prompted, and it was only then she realised she was staring at him.

'Er…sorry.' Slightly flustered, she looked down at Mya's notes, adjusted her glasses, even though they were already perfectly positioned on her nose, and cleared her throat. 'Well, a few months ago, I was in Argentina at a paediatric conference—'

'I remember. You mentioned it on your first day here.'

'Oh? Good. Well, anyway, I bumped into a colleague who's presently conducting a research study into a new drug for asthma sufferers, especially ones who are dependent upon or having reactions to corticosteroids.'

Sean sat up a little straighter in his chair. 'Is that Dr Aloysius Markum?'

'It is.'

'I've just re-read his preliminary findings, which were published in the latest medical journal.'

'Yes.'

'But that study is closed. There's no way we could get Mya onto it and, besides, she'd have to go to Sydney.'

'That's not entirely accurate. The study has new funding to test the drug in different climates to see if there is

any difference. Australia has a great range of tempera-
tures with, for example, places like Tasmania being almost twenty degrees cooler than Adelaide at the same
time of year, which is why he's received approval to expand the study.'

'Do you really think you can get Mya onto the study?'
For the first time in their discussion there was a thread of
hope in Sean's words.

Jane smiled warmly and nodded. 'Ninety-five per cent
sure.' She looked at the clock on the wall, adding on the
half-hour time difference for Sydney. 'He'll be at the hospital now. I'll give him a call.' Without another word she
pulled out her cellphone and dialled Dr Markum's number.

'Hi, Al,' she said a moment later. 'It's Jane. I have a patient for your study.'

Sean watched as she gave Dr Markum Mya's immediate details before saying, 'I have her treating doctor here,
my colleague Sean Booke.' She held her phone out to him
and nodded with encouragement. 'He's interested.'

With that, Sean found himself discussing Mya's treatment with one of Australia's leading specialists in paediatric respiratory disorders, the man Jane Diamond had
simply called 'Al'. Another fifteen minutes and it was all
organised. He was to email through the relevant documen-
tation but Dr Markum seemed more than happy at the idea
of accepting Mya onto his new research study.

'I'll have my assistant email through what you'll need
to discuss with Mya's parents and also the consent forms.
I'm more than happy to talk to the parents either via phone
or internet chat. Oh, and look after our Jane,' Dr Markum
added, without breaking for breath. 'I'm still annoyed Luc
managed to snatch her away from me.'

'I don't follow...' Sean remarked, looking across to

where Jane stood on the ward, chatting with one of their young patients.

'I offered Jane a job when I knew her contract with Edna Robe was almost up. Jane's not only a brilliant doctor but a brilliant woman. She helped my own daughter two years ago to recover from an eating disorder, which leaves me heavily in her debt, so just make sure you look after her while she's there and, hopefully, when her contract expires, she'll finally agree to come back to Sydney and perform her miracles here.'

With that, Dr Markum rang off, leaving Sean holding Jane's cellphone and watching her more closely. She laughed at something the young twelve-year-old boy had said as she straightened his bedsheets, her features radiating pure happiness.

She really was very natural with their patients and to hear such a glowing reference from a man of Dr Markum's repute, as well as the fact that Luc really had head-hunted her, made Sean consider Jane in a new light. During the past weeks he'd been so determined to keep his distance from her, not wanting to discuss or relive anything to do with his past, that he was now beginning to wonder if he hadn't under-estimated the woman Jane Diamond had turned into.

Still, the question remained—why *had* she turned down a man like Aloysius Markum? Surely working at a larger, more prominent hospital in Sydney was a better career move than coming here to Adelaide?

The question stayed with him for the next few weeks and he wondered if he had any right to ask her such a personal question. If he did, would it open the door to them discussing their past? Would it change the calm working relationship they'd managed to create, so much so that she no longer seemed on edge if they were left alone together?

'I see Mya's beginning to improve,' Jane remarked as they came off the ward after an intensive round.

'Are you heading up to the outpatient clinic?' he asked, and she nodded. 'I'll walk with you, if that's all right,' he added.

'Er…of course. We're both going the same way.' She shrugged her shoulders as though everything was perfectly normal.

Where they'd managed to form a calm, professional relationship during her time here, actually walking through the corridors together was something they'd avoided until now. Chatting at the nurses' station? Fine. Discussing patients in outpatient clinic? Necessary. But this? Jane racked her brain for something to say, determined to keep everything strictly on a professional level. She knew she still needed to ask Sean if it was possible for her to see Spencer, to hopefully, in the long term, spend a good deal of time with her nephew, but for the time being she'd been comfortable developing a firm grounding, a professional appreciation, before she hit him with such a request. Even the thought of asking him churned her stomach.

'Um, I'm so pleased Mya's parents were agreeable to her taking part in the study. A lot of people are quite skittish when they hear the words "research project".' She smiled as she spoke.

'It is good to see Mya improving.' Silence reigned, their footsteps echoing in the unusually deserted corridor. 'How's your own research project going?'

'Good. Thanks. Slowly at the moment but I've had two new patients sign up in the last week so that's good news.'

'Yes.'

Silence once more. She should talk more about her research project. That was a neutral topic. 'Actually, the two patients who have signed up are siblings.'

'Is that common?'

'With twins perhaps, but this is a brother and sister, different ages, with different types of eating disorder.'

'What does that tell you? Big trauma in their past?'

'That's the starting point.'

'Are they close? The siblings?'

'Not from our first interview.'

'You and Daina never really got along, did you,' Sean stated rhetorically, the words coming from his mouth before he could think about it.

Jane glanced up at him, a look of disbelief on her face, and when she answered her tone was clipped and brisk. 'No.'

'Why was that, do you think?'

Jane tried to control her rising temper. The one major topic that could easily rile her was the topic of Daina but, she rationalised, she knew that in returning to Adelaide, where Sean and Spencer had now made their home, it would eventually be something she'd have to discuss.

Reminding herself that it was necessary to remain on Sean's good side if she wanted access to Spencer, she tried to control her reaction. Even if she could see her nephew only once a month, that would be terrific. She could get to know him, tell him about the grandparents he'd never known and share some of her better, happier memories with him.

Jane took a steadying breath and paused in the corridor, Sean stopping beside her. 'Jane. I'm sorry, I shouldn't have just blurted out—'

'How well did you know Daina? *Really* know your wife?'

At her question, Sean's expression instantly changed to

one of deep-seated pain before he quickly recovered and replaced his expression with one of benign detachment. 'Ex-wife. We were divorced soon after Spencer was born.'

'Really? I wasn't aware of that.' But she was aware of the bitterness he'd been unable to disguise from his tone. 'So if you know what she was really like, how can you ask me that?'

Sean clenched his jaw and gritted his teeth. 'Whenever I do let myself think of her, I try to remember her the way she was during those first few months of our marriage, before...' He stopped. 'I do it for Spencer.' He shook his head. 'He doesn't need to know the truth about his mother. Not now, at any rate.'

Jane nodded. 'I can understand that because the truth of who Daina really was, of the emotional pain she was capable of inflicting, is just too painful to remember, isn't it?'

'Yes.' His lips barely moved as he spoke, then he exhaled harshly and shook his head. 'Why did you come here, Jane? From what I understand, you had several job offers. Why dredge up all these old emotions? Daina is dead. There's nothing you or I can do to change the past.'

'I don't want to change the past, Sean.'

'Then what *do* you want, Jane?'

'I want to change my future...and I want that future to include Spencer.'

CHAPTER TWO

JANE LET HERSELF into her room, which was situated in the hospital's residential wing. At least she'd managed to obtain a room with an en suite and small kitchenette. At the moment it was ideal, living in such close proximity to the hospital, as it lifted the pressure of finding somewhere more permanent. She could concentrate on her patients and research project and not have to worry about traffic or where to garage a car. There were shops nearby, which provided everything she required, and a good public transport service to assist her if she needed more.

It was now the beginning of February and thanks to daylight saving there was no need for her to turn on the lights, but at the moment she wished the room were in darkness. It was half past seven in the evening and she was exhausted. Not only that, she couldn't believe she'd blurted out her sole purpose for returning to Adelaide to the one man who had total control over her request.

After she'd stated she wanted Spencer to be in her life, Sean had glared at her, his frown returning, before he'd shaken his head and walked away. Trembling with anxiety, Jane had found it almost impossible to shelve her own personal problems enough to concentrate on the clinic, highly conscious of keeping a safe distance from Sean at all times.

However, when she'd been introduced to Tessa, a young

girl of six who she'd ended up admitting due to a bad urinary tract infection, one of the symptoms associated with
eating disorders, Jane had pushed her own issues to the
back of her mind. When the clinic ended, Jane quickly
grabbed a bite to eat from the hospital's cafeteria, before
heading back to the ward to see how Tessa was settling in.

'She's very quiet. Not speaking,' Anthea told her. 'She
didn't want to stay but didn't want to go home either.'

'Hmm.' Jane processed this information. 'OK. Have
the night staff keep a close eye on her and call me if there
are any concerns. I'm staying in the residential wing so I
can come right over.'

'I'll make a note in her file.' Anthea's words had been
soft and the two of them stood there, watching the little
girl, for a few more minutes, Jane's concern rising. With
Tessa being so unsettled, as well as not feeling well because of the urinary tract infection, this first night might
be hard for her.

Now as Jane lay down on the bed, taking off her glasses
and kicking off her shoes, she couldn't ignore the niggling
sensation that there was something going on with Tessa
that no one was aware of. Little girls of six only had eating
disorders if something else was very wrong in their lives.

Her phone started ringing and Jane sluggishly opened
her eyes, reaching out her hand to the nightstand, patting
around until she located it. It was only then she realised
she'd dozed off, still completely dressed and lying on top
of the bed covers.

'Dr Diamond.'

'Oh, uh…Jane, is it?'

'Yes.'

'I'm calling from the ward. There's a note in Tessa's
file to call you if—'

'I'm on my way,' Jane interrupted, as she quickly disconnected the call and hunted around in the now-dark room for her shoes. Collecting her glasses and the hospital lanyard, which contained her hospital pass key as well as the key to her room, Jane headed back to the hospital, smoothing a hand down her hair to ensure it wasn't sticking out all over the place.

'Thanks for coming,' the night sister said. 'Tessa's been lying in her bed, whimpering and crying softly. Every time one of us gets near her, she stops, closes her eyes tight and completely ignores us.'

'OK. Thanks.' Jane nodded politely at the sister before heading to Tessa's bed. Although there were other children in the ward, she didn't want to pull the curtain around Tessa's bed for privacy because if the little girl had been abused in some way, which was the way Jane's intuition was leading her, then the last thing Tessa would want was to have herself 'cut off', as it were, from the rest of the ward.

Instead, Jane walked quietly over to Tessa's bedside, her heart almost breaking at the whimpering sound coming from the child. Just as the night sister had stated, Tessa immediately stopped the instant she realised there was an adult present.

'Hi, Tessa. It's me. Dr Jane. We met before.'

No answer.

'I'm really a bit tired. Do you mind if I sit down here for a minute or two?'

Again no answer.

'Thanks,' she remarked, and sat in the chair beside Tessa's bed. Jane remained silent to begin with then quietly began to sing, her soothing, clear voice audible to the rest of the small ward but not disturbing any of the other patients.

When one song finished, Jane would be quiet for a few

minutes before starting another song. After an hour the night sister quietly walked over, handed Jane a bottle of water, gave her a thumbs-up and a nod of approval before leaving them alone.

Jane gratefully took a sip of the cool water before starting on another song. When she'd finished that one, she settled back in the chair and relaxed.

'Can I hear another one?' a little timid voice asked, when Jane hadn't started the next song for a good five minutes.

Jane's answer was to start singing again. No need for words or questions, the melodious sound of her voice was having a positive effect on Tessa and that was all that mattered. Another hour later Jane couldn't help but smother a yawn, pleased to note that Tessa was now in a deep, relaxed sleep.

Very slowly, Jane stood from the chair, stretching out her tired limbs before heading over to the nurses' station. She wanted to take a closer look at Tessa's case notes, eager to try and find something, anything, that would give her some clues as to what was really going on in the little girl's life.

'That was beautiful,' the night sister said, and Jane smiled her thanks.

'Agreed. I never knew you had such a lovely voice.' The deep words were spoken from directly behind her and Jane spun round, coming face to face with Sean. Unfortunately, she'd moved too quickly, making herself light-headed.

'Whoa.' Sean's arms came around her instantly, for the second time since she'd come back into his life. 'We've really got to stop meeting like this,' he murmured as Jane tried to steady herself. She wasn't sure if it was her imagination or fatigue but she could have sworn Sean's voice seemed kinder, gentler. Was this a good thing? She certainly hoped so. If he could see her for who she was, not just as Daina's sister, then perhaps she stood some chance of him approving her request to see Spencer.

Sean led Jane over to a vacant chair and helped her to sit down, trying to ignore the way her soft sunflowery scent captivated his senses. How could she smell as fresh as a daisy when it was almost six o'clock in the morning?

'I think all your beautiful singing might have drained your oxygen reserves.' The night sister chuckled. 'Although I have to say, you've made the night more pleasant to deal with.'

'That she has,' Sean agreed, immediately stepping back when Jane eased herself away from him, her hands held up in front of her in a defensive manner.

'I'm fine.' She tried not to snap, but it was difficult given she was cross with herself for being far too aware of Sean, of the way his warm hands had caused her to feel safe and secure, even for the briefest of moments. 'But thank you,' she added belatedly.

'At least Tessa's sleeping—*really* sleeping now.' The night sister looked over towards ward room two, where she could hear giggling. 'Which is more than I can say for some of the other children.' With a sigh she left the nurses' station to go and deal with whichever recalcitrant patient dared to be awake at this hour in the morning.

Sean was left alone with Jane but she seemed more than happy to ignore him as she picked up Tessa's file and started reading it. After watching her for a moment, he decided to take a leaf out of her book and began reading his patient files, catching up on the notes the nursing staff had made during the night. If Jane wanted to play the professional card, so could he. They would sit there, ignore each other and do their work. The fact that he'd known her since she was a teenager, the fact that he'd been married to her older sister, the fact that her sister had ripped his heart out, cut it into tiny pieces and then set fire to them, in reality, had nothing at all to do with Jane.

And yet…he didn't seem able to keep his curiosity levels in check. She'd said she wanted to get to know Spencer. Why? Why *now*? Was she dying? Had something terrible happened to her…again? Sean closed his eyes on the thought. He knew all about the accident that had taken Jane's and Daina's parents from them, Daina annoyed that she'd been thrust into the role of responsible adult to care for her thirteen-year-old sister.

Jane had looked directly at him, her intent clear when she'd asked, 'How well did you know Daina? *Really* know your wife?' and he'd felt as though she'd slapped him. There was so much about his marriage that he'd shoved aside, promising himself never to think about it but with Jane returning, infiltrating his world, that resolve was becoming difficult to control.

Sean opened his eyes, glancing surreptitiously at Jane. Had her hair been that long, that deep chocolaty brown in colour, that silky, all those years ago? He clenched his hand into a fist to stop himself from wanting to reach out and run his fingers through it, wondering if it really was as glorious as it appeared.

He needed to stop thinking about Jane, to control his thoughts. She'd asked him how well he'd known his wife, and to begin with he had to admit he'd thought he'd known Daina fairly well…until he'd discovered, thanks to an ex-friend's guilty conscience, the number of other men who had also 'known Daina fairly well'. That confession had come after Spencer's traumatic birth and Sean, in his stubbornness, had insisted on a DNA test to reassure himself that Spencer was indeed his. Thankfully, Daina had been telling the truth for once and from that moment on Sean had devoted his attention and energies towards his baby son, rather than towards his wayward, cheating wife, serving her with divorce papers as soon as possible.

'Would you stop staring at me, please?'

Jane's voice cut through his thoughts and it was only then that Sean realised he was doing exactly what she'd accused him of. Her green eyes bored into his and he quickly looked down at the case notes in his hands. 'Er…sorry.'

Jane sighed heavily before returning her attention to Tessa's case notes, flicking back through the pages again, intent on reading everything possible about every admission, right back to her birth.

'Looking for anything in particular?' he asked.

'I'll know it when I see it.'

'Determined, eh?'

'And stubborn.'

'I'm sure those qualities have served you well over the years.'

Jane lifted her head and glared at him for a moment. 'What's that supposed to mean?'

Sean raised his eyebrows at her tone and when he looked into her eyes he was a little surprised to see them filled with repressed fire. 'You're…angry with me?' He searched her gaze again to ensure he'd read her emotion correctly.

Jane merely rolled her eyes at his words and returned her focus to the paperwork before her. 'Haven't you learnt not to tease women when they're frustrated because they can't find the answer to the problem plaguing them?'

'Er…actually, I have learnt that lesson, seeing as I have younger twin sisters, but sometimes, Jane, it's difficult to resist.'

Jane raised her head and stared at him for a moment. 'You have sisters?' Then, before he could answer, she shook her head as though to clear it from unnecessary distractions and returned her attention to the notes. 'There has to be something in here, some event, some incident, even a small one, that was enough to cause these disruptions in Tessa's life.'

'Disruptions?'

Jane stretched out her hand towards where Tessa was now sleeping soundly. 'She doesn't eat, she doesn't sleep, she whimpers any time an adult comes near her at night.'

'You think she might have been abused by an adult?'

'That's the most common assumption but it may not necessarily be an adult. She's scared, not of the dark but of the night.'

'What's the difference?'

Jane breathed in deeply, her eyes flashing with fire, and Sean could see her hackles were beginning to rise. He immediately held up one hand to stop her tirade before she began. 'I'm not teasing or trying to be difficult, Jane. I haven't had the training or life experiences you've had. I'm only enquiring because I don't understand your statement. Nothing more. I'm as concerned about Tessa as you are. Perhaps, if we head to the cafeteria and grab a cup of coffee, we can make some sense of the situation.'

Jane immediately shook her head. 'I'm happy where I am, thank you.' The last thing she wanted was to be sitting in close proximity to Sean in an almost deserted hospital cafeteria, listening to the sultry sound of his voice. It was bad enough that the night sister had left them alone at the nurses' station, forcing Jane to erect her automatic defences.

She'd had to protect herself from so much over the years, just like Tessa was doing now, not from physical or sexual abuse but from verbal and emotional abuse, which were every bit as damaging as the others. There had been one particular side to Daina only Jane had been privy to...

and she couldn't stop the niggling question in the back of her mind as to whether or not Sean had also seen that side of her sister.

'Fair enough. In that case, would you mind explaining your statement? Why would Tessa be afraid of the night and not of the dark? I always thought the two were synonymous.'

'Look at the ward,' Jane invited. 'There are lights on. Small nightlights. It's not dark, not pitch black. Tessa's not afraid of the dark because that's where she feels the safest. It's dark in her mind, she can curl up into a corner in a dark room and no one will ever find her, but night-time… there's a real fear associated with that because the majority of people sleep at night and sleeping is when a person is most vulnerable.'

'You're saying that night-time makes her feel vulnerable?'

'Yes. How many times have you heard people saying they just wished for the night to be over, that they couldn't wait for the first rays of sunlight to start seeping through into the day? Insomniacs feel it all the time. All those hours they just lie there, not sleeping, just waiting. In Tessa's case, whatever has happened to her happens at night, which is why she refuses to sleep, which is why she whimpers, filled with anticipatory dread at what might or might not happen.'

'The mind is a powerful thing.'

'Most definitely.' Jane's voice was soft as she sighed, her previous annoyance having vanished as she once more stared down at Tessa's case notes.

'Do you want me to have a look?'

Jane handed them over without a word before standing and walking towards the edge of the ward where she watched Tessa sleep, the little girl's breathing still calm and relaxed. 'I wonder if this is the first decent sleep she's had in…well, I don't know how long.'

She continued to stand there while Sean read through Tessa's entire file. 'You're right. There's nothing that stands out.' Jane's shoulders slumped dejectedly at this news. 'But I do have a suggestion.'

'I'm open to it.'

'Why not task a few medical students to do a case study on Tessa?'

Jane raised an eyebrow at this. 'Go on.'

'For the next forty-eight hours they are to unobtrusively observe Tessa, her parents, her siblings, her friends—anyone and everyone who comes into contact with her, including all hospital staff, whether male or female, and also any interaction with other patients. I see you've already requested she have a consult with the dietician and the hospital's child psychologist, so once we have the data from the students, we can organise a conference and really see if we can't get to the bottom of this.'

'Wouldn't we need the parents' permission?'

'The medical students aren't treating Tessa, they're observing her. Tessa has been admitted to the hospital for observation as well as treatment for her urinary tract infection. Tessa wouldn't be a part of any sort of research study, she's just being observed in the interest of her health.'

Jane turned from watching Tessa and looked at Sean. 'I'll speak to Luc, and I'd also like her taken off the ward round during this time.'

'Agreed.' He nodded. 'It's a plan.'

'Yes. Yes, it is.' Jane couldn't believe how much lighter her heart felt now that there was a way forward, a way to hopefully figure out whatever was hurting Tessa. 'Thank you, Sean.'

He smiled at her then, a full-blown, twinkling-eyed

smile that somehow pierced the barrier she'd so carefully constructed around her heart and flooded her world with light. She immediately returned to her seat, dropping down into the chair before her knees refused to support her weight due to the fact that they'd turned to jelly. Boy, oh, boy, Sean Booke's smile was lethal! 'You're more than welcome, Jane.'

He didn't seem to notice the effect he was having on her. Such a smile should be outlawed. The action had completely changed his features from ones she'd always considered to be dark and brooding to pure handsome sensuality.

When the night sister returned, Jane was more than thankful that Sean's attention was diverted as he asked about the patients who had been playing up but Jane didn't listen to half of what they were saying. She was still trying to gain control over her senses, swallowing over her suddenly dry mouth and fervently trying to quell the multitude of proverbial butterflies presently going haywire in her stomach.

No man...not even her ex-fiancé...had ever affected her in such a way. Things like this simply didn't happen to her. She wasn't the romantic, girly, lovey-dovey type so why had she been this affected by one simple smile from a man she wasn't even sure she liked?

'I know it's almost time for the ward to wake up and I'll make sure Tessa's not disturbed for as long as possible,' the night sister was saying, 'but I also think you need to get some rest, Dr Diamond. You're not due back on the ward until eight o'clock, so head over to the residential wing now and try to get some sleep.'

'You're staying in the res wing?' For some reason this news surprised Sean.

'Yes. It's convenient.'

'For the moment.'

Jane shrugged. 'I have no problem staying there for the rest of the year.' She looked over at Tessa, who was still sleeping soundly. 'You'll—'

'Call you if there are any problems,' Sister interrupted, nodding her head. 'Absolutely.'

'I'll walk you over,' Sean stated, rising to his feet.

'It's fine. You don't have to do that.'

'It's a safety thing.'

For who? Jane wanted to ask, because even the thought of having Sean close to her as they walked through the quiet hospital was disconcerting enough for her. She gingerly stood, pleased to discover her legs were now going to support her. She looked from Sister to Sean, realising there was no way out. It was easier to accept.

'Right,' Sister continued. 'You two are organised, so off you go. I'd best go and receive updates from the rest of my staff before the breakfast trolleys are brought up.'

Sean swept a hand in front of his body, indicating Jane should precede him. 'Shall we?'

It was easier for her to accept his offer than to kick up a stink because she knew if that was the case, she'd have to explain exactly *why* she was kicking up a stink and the last thing she wanted to say to Sean Booke right now was that she found his spicy scent rather intoxicating.

Neither of them spoke as they walked through the deserted corridors, heading to the rear of the hospital towards the residential wing. Even after they'd entered the res wing and Jane had signed in, Sean still insisted on accompanying her right up to her room. The clerk behind the desk in the foyer was watching them intently and once more Jane decided it was easier to go with the flow than argue. She gritted her teeth, desperately trying to ignore her awareness of Sean's close proximity, and started for the stairwell. It wasn't until the door had closed behind them, their footsteps echoing around them, that Sean spoke.

'Jane?'

'Yes.'

'You mentioned that you wanted to change your future and that you wanted Spencer to be a part of that future.'

Jane swallowed over the sudden lump forming in her throat before answering, 'Yes.' Was this it? Was she going to find out that he didn't want her to see Spencer whilst walking up a flight of stairs in the residential wing? He didn't say anything else until she'd pushed open the door to the floor she was staying on. It was difficult for her to resist the urge to run the rest of the way, to disappear into the safety of her room before Sean asked the question she could feel was coming.

'Why now?' he asked, as they stopped outside her door.

Gathering her courage, Jane turned to face him, shrugging one shoulder.

'You're not sick, are you? Terminally ill? Or discovered you have some strange hereditary disease that Spencer might also inherit?'

That was not what she'd expected him to say and she couldn't help the way her lips curved upwards slightly in surprise. 'No. I'm not sick, or dying of some hereditary disease. Spencer is safe.'

Sean exhaled slowly and nodded. 'Good.'

Jane continued to stand there, waiting for him to ask another question, but none came. The awkwardness of the moment started to increase and she was very self-conscious about them both standing there and saying nothing. With jerky, almost robotic movements she pressed the electronic keycard on her lanyard against the door to open it. Sean still didn't ask her anything else.

'OK, then. I guess I'll see you later on this morning.

Thanks for walking me over.' She pushed open the door, eager to escape the awkwardness, but Sean put his hand on her arm, stopping her.

'Jane. You didn't answer my question.'

She turned to look at him, her skin still warm from his touch even after he'd removed his hand. She wasn't used to being touched, especially not by handsome, brooding men such as the one who stood before her. She swallowed and slowly raised her gaze to meet his.

'Why did I come back now?' He nodded as she repeated his question. 'Well...' she faltered, before shrugging and deciding it was better just to be honest. 'Because...I've reached the end of me.'

He stared at her in puzzlement and she realised she needed to expand on her answer. The last thing she wanted to do was to completely bare her soul, to reveal to him just how lonely she was, but if she wanted to see Spencer then perhaps it was inevitable that she at least give him some information. She looked down at the floor and drew in a deep breath before meeting his gaze once more, her words rushing out quickly.

'I have nothing else, Sean. No one else.' She spread her hands wide in a gesture of openness. 'I've tried to fill my life with work and my patients and my colleagues and for a while there I thought I might actually be successful. I was even engaged for a short time, hopeful I'd be able to forget my past, to somehow pretend I was someone else.' She shook her head. 'I was wrong. Eamon...er...my fiancé, told me I never really opened up to him, always kept a part of myself hidden, secret, and he was absolutely right.

'It's been over twelve months since he broke our engagement, telling me I wasn't the woman he wanted any more, and during that time I finally realised that if I'm ever going to have any hope of a normal life, I need not only to address my past but to make peace with it. I hoped by focusing on the good things, like getting to know Spencer—my only blood relative left in the world—that I might actually come out of this journey in one piece.'

Jane looked down at the floor, annoyed that her voice had broken on the final words. She'd been doing so well, especially as being this candid with someone she really didn't know a lot about was extremely difficult.

Pursing her lips together in an effort to control the tears she could feel pricking at the backs of her eyes, she breathed out slowly and forced herself to meet his gaze. 'I have no one, Sean. No parents, no grandparents, no aunts or uncles. No cousins and...no sister. I've tried everything I can to find some level of happiness in my life but I've reached the end...and coming here was the only other option left.' She sniffed, her eyes now brimming with tears, and when one fell from her lashes, she impatiently brushed it away, not wanting to guilt him into feeling sorry for her. She didn't want his pity, she wanted his understanding and, hopefully, his permission to allow her access to Spencer.

'I have nothing else,' she whispered, before being unable to control herself any longer and quickly disappearing into the safety of her room, closing the door behind her.

CHAPTER THREE

JANE WASN'T SURE how she was going to face Sean after the way she'd all but blurted out her sad sob story, cried and then shut the door in his face. There was no way he was going to allow her access to Spencer now that he realised just how unglued she was. Worst of all, he might think she was like Daina, unstable deep down inside.

She wasn't. She'd worked hard to be nothing like her older sister, who had been manipulative, arrogant and, at times, downright cruel. Jane tried to close her thoughts to the memories that infiltrated her mind, memories she'd worked so hard to shield. Daina whispering in her ear that no one would ever love her because she was a scarred freak. Daina looking at Jane's high-school transcript and calling her weird because normal people didn't get top marks in every subject. Daina ignoring her, for weeks on end, pretending she didn't exist.

That had been the worst one of all. Daina had legally been Jane's guardian. They'd only had each other so when her sister had ignored her, not speaking to her or acknowledging her for long periods of time, the young teenage Jane had become very distraught.

More often than not, Jane would end up in her bedroom, sitting in the corner convinced there was something wrong with *her*. Then, out of the blue, Daina would change. She'd hug and kiss her little sister, cuddle her, tell her that everything would be all right. She'd take Jane out and lavish her with attention, buying her clothes and make-up and trinkets; they'd go to the movies and play games at the arcade. Jane had lived for those days, wondering whenever she went to the kitchen each morning to prepare breakfast for them both whether *this* would be the good day, the day where nice Daina came to visit.

Back then, her sister's erratic behaviour had definitely affected her but as soon as Daina had up and married Sean, leaving Jane all alone, she'd realised the only way to really deal with her sister and to avoid the negative effects had been to shut Daina out of her life as much as possible.

It had been clear, just from seeing Sean's expression when she'd asked him about how well he'd known his wife, that Daina had hurt him, too. Both of them had been left emotionally scarred and she accepted the fact that Sean would do anything and everything to protect Spencer. If he thought she was like Daina, there was no way he'd allow her to form any sort of attachment to the boy…and she couldn't blame him.

'Sean.' Jane spoke his name out loud and slowly shook her head from side to side. The fact that she found herself constantly thinking about her ex-brother-in-law was a little disconcerting but, she rationalised, there was a lot at stake. Spencer was important to her and at the moment she'd do almost anything to prove to Sean that she was a calm and controlled adult in the hope that he would give her permission to get to know her nephew.

She didn't want to think about the way Sean's powerful presence had turned her knees to jelly or the way his amazing smile had caused her insides to flutter or the way his blue eyes could be so incredibly expressive. She could simply sit and stare into them all day long and never get bored—and that realisation in itself was enough to startle her.

Any sort of romantic entanglement—with anyone— was the furthest thing from her mind and, besides, Sean was also her colleague for the next twelve months and if dating Eamon had taught her one major lesson, it was to never date colleagues.

She stared at her reflection in the small mirror above the bathroom sink as she slipped her glasses into place. 'Professional persona in place. Time to get to work. Focus on your patients and give them the best care possible. Do *not* think about Sean Booke and the way he can make your knees go weak with just one smile!' Her words and expression were stern and with a firm nod she turned and collected her hospital lanyard and phone from the bed-side dresser.

Breathing in an air of professionalism, Jane left her room and headed back over to the hospital. She couldn't help but look around her, doing a double-take on any man who was six feet four inches tall and had short dark brown hair and blue eyes. Sean was the last person she needed to bump into right now, especially after she'd given herself such strict instructions to the contrary. Thankfully, she didn't bump into him and when she arrived on the ward she headed over to see Tessa.

The little girl was sitting up in bed, doing a jigsaw puzzle and not really wanting to talk or interact with anyone.

'Good morning, Tessa.' Jane smiled and wasn't surprised she didn't receive a response from the girl. 'You've made a good start on that puzzle. Can I help?'

Tessa's answer was to shrug her shoulders but she didn't send Jane away neither did she lose interest in the puzzle.

'Which piece should I put in?' she asked, her fingers hovering over a few of the pieces. She waited a moment, pretending to be unable to choose, and when she finally picked up a piece, Tessa still didn't speak. 'Where does this one go?'

Again, there was no verbal interaction but Jane could see Tessa's gaze darting to exactly where the piece should go. Jane placed it in the right position and smiled. 'There.'

Tessa looked at Jane for a long moment, her brown eyes so deep and expressive, but only for a second. With a blink of her eyes the shutters came down but not before Jane had glimpsed that silent plea for help.

'I *am* going to help you, Tessa,' she told the girl quietly, her voice filled with promise. She also told Tessa that the doctors wouldn't be stopping at her bed during the ward round. 'They'd all want to help you with your jigsaw puzzle,' she said with a small laugh. 'All of us, the other doctors and the nurses and other people you might see while you're here, we *all* like to help people and we all want to help you.' Jane's smile was one of comfort and reassurance. Tessa's response was to look at her for another long moment, shutters still firmly in place, before returning her attention to the puzzle.

When Jane made her way back to the nurses' station, it was to find Luc talking to Sean. 'Good morning,' she murmured, glancing momentarily in Sean's direction, a little surprised at the way her heart rate started to increase. Why was she so aware of him?

'Did you get some rest, Jane?'

'Er...' She couldn't believe how flustered she felt at what would ordinarily be a normal question from any other member of staff but when Sean asked it, it was as though he really was interested, that he really cared. 'Yes. Thank you.'

'Good. And how's Tessa doing?'

'Silently begging for help,' Jane replied softly.

Anthea had just walked into the nurses' station as Jane spoke and the sister sighed with compassion at this news. 'The poor lamb.'

Luc shook his head. 'There's clearly something else going on,' he stated. 'Sean's been telling me about the plan to have some medical students observe Tessa for a few days.'

Jane nodded, her heart rate settling down now that they were talking about work. 'If we can figure out what's going on at home, we'll be one giant step closer to getting Tessa the correct help. That's one of the main focuses with eating disorders. Sometimes all the signs and symptoms point one way yet everything is the opposite. Monitoring Tessa's reaction to everyone who comes into contact with her will go a long way to hopefully providing us with that information.'

Luc pointed to Tessa's case notes on the desk in front of him. 'I read she had a difficult night, although it says she managed a few hours' deep sleep this morning, thanks to…' Luc picked up the case notes and read what the night sister had written '…"to…Dr Diamond's singing"?'

Sean immediately smiled at Jane, speaking before she had the opportunity. 'She has an incredible voice. It soothed more people in the ward than just young Tessa.'

'Oh, I know *all* about Jane's beautiful singing, especially when she sings in French,' Luc remarked, winking at her. Jane ignored Luc's comment and instead tried to figure out her reaction to Sean and why his easygoing smile had caused her body to explode with tingles. She dropped her gaze down to where his tie was perfectly knotted, a bright coloured tie with popular cartoon characters on it, which was sure to delight the children.

Perhaps if she didn't look at his perfect mouth she wouldn't be as affected, but instead she became more

aware of his Adam's apple moving up and down his perfect throat and how her peripheral vision clearly regis-
tered the width of his broad shoulders. Her senses were
all too aware of his smooth, deep voice washing yet another wave of tingles over her. He'd spoken, asked her a
question, and yet, due to his nearness, she had absolutely
no clue what he'd said.

'Hmm?' Jane swallowed, forcing herself to move away
from his overwhelming presence, needing distance, needing to control her rising panic. 'Er...' She couldn't believe
how flustered she felt. 'Um...what did you say, Sean?' She
picked up Tessa's case notes, holding them in front, using
them as some sort of shield. When she dared to glance
at him once more, it was to find him frowning in slight
puzzlement.

'I...' He looked from her to Luc then back again, before
shaking his head. 'It's fine.'

'OK. Well, I think I'll go and pore over Tessa's notes
in the conference room before ward round starts,' Jane
said to no one in particular, before hightailing it out of the
small secluded area, which had made her far too aware of
Sean's presence.

She entered the conference room, unable to believe the
way Sean's nearness, his presence, his voice, his...every-
thing was turning her into a tongue-tied schoolgirl, much
as she'd been when they'd first met all those years ago.

After taking a few deep breaths, she walked over to one
of the chairs at the back of the room and sat down, opening Tessa's notes.

'Why didn't you say something before?' Sean remarked
as he stalked into the conference room, heading directly
towards her and stopping close to where she sat.

Slightly startled, Jane looked up from the case notes.
'Sorry?'

'Luc.'

'What about Luc?'

'You…and *him*.'

'I'm not sure I understand.'

'*You* and *Luc*. You told me you'd moved to Adelaide solely because of Spencer.'

Jane's eyes widened as she grasped his meaning and quickly shook her head. Her glasses slid down her nose and it wasn't until she went to push them back that she realised her hand was trembling a little. 'What? Me and Luc? No. We're friends. Colleagues. Sean, I'm not involved with Luc.'

'It certainly looks that way.'

'It does?'

'You're very…chummy and it's clear he likes you.'

'What?' Jane frowned, positive Sean had the wrong end of the stick. 'Luc is a colleague and a friend.' She spread her hands wide, desperate for him to believe her.

'So why did Dr Markum tell me that Luc managed to persuade you to come and work in Adelaide?'

'Perhaps because Luc *did* manage to persuade me to come and work here.'

'So he could be close to you?'

'What? No.' Jane was confused how things had become so muddled. 'So I could be close to Spencer.'

Sean opened his mouth to say something then closed it again, thinking for a moment. 'But…that implies that Luc knew you and I had a personal connection.'

Jane nodded. 'Yes.'

Sean scratched his forehead. 'How?'

'One night, when we were working together in Paris…' She stopped and started again. 'It was a terrible night. There'd been a multiple MVA and a family of six, four children, two parents, had all been admitted. Both parents

passed away and two of the children. It was horrible, having to tell those two kids—one nine and one fourteen—
that the rest of their family had died.'

'That is terrible.' Sean pulled up a chair and sat down
next to her, his previous annoyance dissipating.

'Afterwards, Luc and I started talking about our families. He told me about his brother, Pierre, and his sister,
Nicolette, and her husband, Stephen. He told me about his
nieces and nephews, his aunts and uncles and I, for all in-
tents and purposes, had no one.' She shrugged as she said
the words. 'No parents, no aunts or uncles or cousins.'

'How long ago was this?'

'Just before Daina passed away.' Jane looked down at
her hands, which were clenched tightly together. 'I told
Luc about a nephew I'd never seen and I must have mentioned your name because he remembered it. So when the
job here came up, Spencer became the cherry Luc needed
to secure my services here at the hospital.'

'You're just friends.'

'Friends,' she agreed.

'I didn't mean to jump to conclusions.'

'Would it matter, though?'

'What? If you were dating Luc?'

'Or anyone else, for that matter. Would it impact your
decision regarding my request to spend time with Spencer?'

'It might. It would depend on who you were dating and
whether or not that relationship might inadvertently affect Spencer.'

Jane nodded, thinking through his words before sitting
forward in her chair and meeting his gaze. 'I am not Daina,
you know. I am nothing like my sister and I hope you can
see that.' Her words were imploring. 'I would never do
anything to hurt Spencer and indeed...' she sat up a little

straighter in her chair, her green eyes flashing with determination and strength '...I would do everything in my power to protect him.'

There was something about the way she spoke, about the way she'd said the word 'protect', that caused Sean to think there was a lot more she *wasn't* saying. She would protect Spencer. Why would Jane think Spencer needed protecting?

Jane's cellphone beeped and she checked the message. 'It's the child psychologist about Tessa. I might not be available for the ward round this morning.'

'I'll let Luc know.'

'Thanks.' Jane stood and gathered her files. 'I hope we're clearer about a few things now, Sean.'

He nodded and with that he watched her walk from the room, head held high, her long plait swishing from side to side as she moved. How was it possible her green eyes could look so...intense? Didn't she have any idea just how passionate she looked when she was determined?

She'd been absolutely correct at guessing his response to her easygoing relationship with Luc. The way the two of them interacted so naturally—which, of course, they would do if, as she'd said, they'd spent a fair amount of time working with each other in the past—had indeed reminded him of the way Daina would flirt and tease with other men.

Jane had clearly realised the track his thoughts had taken and she'd called him on it, indicating she was not only intuitive but direct. From what he'd seen during the past month, she wasn't anything like Daina but, then, Daina had done an excellent job of deceiving him for quite some time.

Jane hadn't been deceptive, though. She hadn't tried to go behind his back and find out information about Spencer. Instead, she'd told him directly that she was hoping for access to his son...and yet he was finding it difficult to trust her.

In fact, he found it difficult to trust any woman, especially one he was attracted to, after the way Daina had treated him.

Attracted? Was he attracted to Jane?

There was no doubt that she had a certain...style to her, one that he was sure many people had underestimated, just as he'd done. She'd shown herself to be highly intelligent as well as caring, two qualities he admired. She definitely didn't tailor her wardrobe, as Daina had, his ex-wife often wearing outfits that he'd considered far too alluring out in public. Was that why Jane dressed the way she did? To prove to herself that she *was* the opposite of Daina?

As the day progressed, Sean found himself unable to stop thinking about what Jane had said about being all alone. Was it true? Did she really have no other family? None?

Daina had never really spoken of any other relatives, except Jane, and even then she'd almost ignored her younger sister's existence, much preferring to concentrate on herself. The thought stayed with him at the back of his mind during outpatients, his sub-committee meetings and even while he was driving home. What was it like to be all alone?

When he pulled into the two-storey house where he lived with his parents and his son, Sean imagined what it might be like to arrive home to a dark, empty home with no one waiting inside. As he scooped Spencer into his arms and tickled the boy's tummy, as he chatted with his parents, who had always been there to help him look after his son, Sean felt such enormous pangs of pain at the thought of all these wonderful people being taken from him.

How would he feel if that extended to his twin sisters and their families? His grandparents? His aunts, uncles and cousins? The emptiness, the void, the loneliness that would be left in his life would consume him. Was that what had happened to Jane?

'Are you all right?' his mother, Louise, asked him as she joined him in the bathroom while he checked his son's teeth.

'Hmm? Sure.' He kept his attention off his mother and on his son. 'There you go, bud. Rinse and spit, wipe your mouth and go and choose some stories for us to read.'

'Yep. 'K, Dad.' Spencer did as he was told while Sean tried not to let his mother see that anything was wrong. Even the briefest thought about losing the people he loved so very much was making him feel uneasy and as Spencer raced from the bathroom, Sean dipped his head and pressed a kiss to his mother's cheek.

'Thanks, Mum.'

'For?' she asked, a little surprised by his action.

'Everything. Being a great mother and grandmother. Always supportive.' He shrugged, feeling highly self-conscious but glad he was saying these words to her.

'Of course.' Louise eyed him cautiously. 'Sean? What's going on?'

Sean raked a hand through his hair and looked past her to make sure Spencer wasn't within earshot. 'Do you remember meeting Daina's sister?'

'Er...Jane?'

'That's it.'

'I spoke to her at the funeral. It was odd. She didn't seem all that upset about her sister's death but at the same time she was very sad.' Louise shook her head. 'I can't explain it.'

'That's probably because she and Daina didn't exactly get along.'

'Not surprising.' His mother's tone was flat, both of them clearly understanding what wasn't being said—that it had been difficult for *anyone* to really get along with Daina.

'Jane's working at the hospital.'

'Your hospital?'

He nodded. 'She's a paediatrician.'

'Oh, yes. I remembered her saying she was a doctor.' Louise frowned. 'Why? What does she want?'

'To see—'

'Daddy!' Spencer called out brightly. 'I'm ready for stories now.'

'Spencer?' Louise guessed. 'She wants to see Spencer?'

'Yes.'

'Are you going to let her? Can you trust her?'

Sean shrugged as he headed towards his son's room, the image of Jane seated beside Tessa's bed, her sweet, angelic voice filling the air. He could recall the song she'd been singing and how it had made not only Tessa but the night staff feel. Surely someone whose intention it was to help others could be trusted just a little bit. Right? Besides, Jane would accept any time he would allow her to spend with Spencer. She was leaving it up to him decide and orchestrate. Surely that was a good thing. Right?

'Can you trust her?' Louise repeated, and Sean met his mother's gaze.

'I hope so.'

The next day, Sean had firmly decided he was going to allow Jane limited access to Spencer to begin with.

'Are you sure?' his mother had asked when he'd informed her of his decision.

'Yes. Jane is very different to Daina and, besides, you've seen the gifts she's sent Spencer every year for his birthday and at Christmas.'

'They're always his favourite,' Louise agreed.

'Although he has no idea who this "Aunty Jane" person is, he's always enjoyed the presents she's sent.'

'What will you tell him?'

'The truth. She's his mother's sister and she's moved to Adelaide.' With the decision firmly made, Sean started to imagine what Jane's expression might be like when he told her the good news. Would she be excited? Happy? Apprehensive? Worried?

Ever since she'd told him about being so incredibly lonely, Sean had wanted to remove that forlorn look from her eyes. He hoped his affirmative answer would accomplish this. How could any person really be filled with sorrow and yet still have the strength to keep on going, to keep on forging ahead, making a difference in other people's lives? The thought of him being able to make a difference in *Jane*'s life filled him with a sense of happiness he hadn't felt in a very long time, and as he arrived at the hospital he decided to find Jane and tell her the news immediately.

He grinned to himself as he entered the ward, an extra spring in his step as he headed to the nurses' station, but much to his chagrin Romana informed him that Jane had already been in to see her patients and had left.

'Oh.' Sean was disappointed. 'Do you know where she is? We don't have clinic today so I'm not quite sure where I can find her.'

'Are you looking for Jane?' Luc asked as he came onto the ward.

'Yes.'

'She's in the research labs all morning.'

'Huh.' Sean frowned and Luc picked up the phone receiver on the desk and handed it to Sean.

'Call her.'

Sean looked from his friend to the phone and back again, catching the very interested look in Luc's eyes. 'It's OK. I'll catch up with her later. It's no big deal.'

But it was, he told himself as he sat in his small office and worked steadily through his pile of paperwork. He had news, important news that would make Jane smile. The longer he couldn't pass on the news, the more urgent his need became. He had it in his power to see her green eyes shining with happiness rather than sadness.

Feeling as though the walls of his office were starting to close in on him, he stalked out of the department and out into the hot Adelaide sunshine. It was a scorcher of a day and he rolled up the sleeves of his white shirt, immediately missing the air-conditioning, as he headed towards the North Adelaide shopping district.

It was only as he noticed the increase of people in the area that he realised it was lunchtime and as he hadn't yet eaten he decided that would be next on his list. It might even improve his disposition. He wasn't the sort of man who liked to be at odds with himself and he'd been that way far too often in the past.

Marrying Daina had most certainly taken him out of his comfort zone and although their marriage had been far from smooth, he'd gained a son from the union. Spencer was a constant source of delight and blessings and Sean knew how fortunate he was to have such a wonderful child.

'Sean. Mate. Good to see you,' came the friendly greeting from Ronan, the proprietor of the café Sean preferred to frequent. 'Usual table?' Ronan didn't even bother to collect a menu as Sean knew the selection off by heart.

'Oops. Sorry, mate. Looks as though someone's already sitting at your table.'

'Never mind. By the win—' Sean stopped as he saw exactly who was seated at his table. His grin widened and he unconsciously straightened the knot of his tie. 'Actually, Ronan, don't worry about it. My usual table looks… just perfect.'

There, sipping a cup of coffee while reading a toy catalogue from a nearby toy shop, sat the one woman he'd spent all morning wanting to talk to.

CHAPTER FOUR

'HELLO, JANE.'

Jane looked up from poring over the toy catalogue directly into the face of Sean Booke.

'Sean?'

'I've been looking for you,' he remarked as he pulled out the chair opposite her and sat down. Jane shifted in her seat, sitting up a little straighter.

'Oh?' She immediately pulled her cellphone out of her pocket to check if she had any missed calls.

'I didn't leave a message. Luc said you were in the research labs so I didn't want to bother you.'

'But the patients are all right? Tessa?'

'The patients are fine.' He was impressed at just how much she really cared about them. 'I hope you don't mind me joining you.' He was calm and polite. 'Have you ordered any food yet?'

She frowned at him, unsure what he wanted. Why had he been looking for her? Had he reached a decision regarding Spencer? Did he have more questions?

'Er…no.'

Sean put his arm in the air to get Ronan's attention. The proprietor came over. 'Ready to order?'

Sean looked at Jane. 'Antipasto and another coffee?' he asked, and before she could think what she was doing,

Jane had nodded her consent, rationalising that if she was nibbling on some food, perhaps it might assist her with not being so distracted by every little move the man opposite her made.

'Antipasto for two and coffees,' Ronan confirmed, before nodding. 'I'll see to it immediately.'

'Thank you, Sean,' she said, once they were alone again. 'I guess eating something isn't such a bad idea, especially as I want to spend some time with Tessa this afternoon before the meeting to go over the medical students' preliminary results.'

'What's your gut telling you?' he asked.

Jane shrugged. 'A few different things.'

'Do you trust your instincts or do you prefer to deal with cold data and facts to make your decisions?'

'Both.'

Sean grinned. 'Me too.'

They continued to discuss a few more patients, Jane determined to keep the conversation nice and professional for the moment so she could regain control over her wayward senses. Sean had the ability to shatter her usual calm. It wasn't just his good looks and charm, it was the way he genuinely seemed to care for others, not only the patients but the staff as well. In fact, just last week she'd overheard him talking to Romana, reassuring the nurse, who'd been upset because her dog had been ill.

'Did you take him to the vet I recommended?' Sean had asked gently.

'Yes. He was very nice, very caring.'

'He's a good vet.'

'I know. I'm just worried.'

'He'll take care of little Kelad,' he'd promised, his tone so absolute there was no way even Jane had doubted him and, thankfully, Romana had come in just a few days later and announced that little Kelad was much better.

With the arrival of their food and drinks, she was glad, not only of the delicious morsels before her, only then realising just how hungry she was, but also the welcome distraction eating provided. Sitting opposite Sean, seeing him away from the hospital setting, sharing a plate of food with him, Jane found herself becoming more and more intrigued by him. With his dark hair and blue eyes, he was still as incredibly handsome as she remembered and she wondered whether he had a girlfriend or partner. Had he been able to move on to a more successful and healthy relationship after his disastrous marriage?

If she knew he was involved with someone else, it might help her to curb the increasing desire she felt for him… but how did she ask him such a thing without it becoming awkward, especially when they seemed to have only just found a more even footing to build on?

Sean pointed to the toy catalogue beside her on the table as he swallowed his mouthful. 'Looking at investing in some new toys?'

Jane flicked her fingers over the pages and smiled. 'Actually, I was hoping to get some ideas for Spencer. It's only seven weeks until his birthday.'

'Yes, but you don't have to factor in posting time this year. You can give him your present in person.'

'I can?' Jane shifted in her seat, sitting up a little straighter at this news.

'Jane.' He put his knife and fork down before looking at her. 'First of all, I'd like to apologise for questioning you about Luc. Even if anything was going on, it still wouldn't have been any of my business.'

Jane stared at him, blinking once then twice.

'What is it?' he asked, when he realised she was looking at him with a confused expression.

'I...just hadn't expected you to be so—' She quickly
stopped what she saying and looked down at her hands.

'To be so...what?' he probed, the small curve returning to the edge of his mouth. 'So...gracious?' Jane stared
at him. 'So...reasonable?' Jane's lips began to twitch into
the beginnings of a smile. 'So...perfunctory?'

Jane's smile increased as she slowly shook her head
from side to side. 'So *honest*.' Good heavens. When this
man turned on the charm, he *turned on the charm*!

Sean gave her a quizzical look. 'You hadn't expected
me to be honest?'

Jane spread her hands wide. 'Our few dealings in the
past haven't always been the most straightforward.'

'True, but hopefully we've managed to clear the air a
little.' He gestured to the empty plates before them. 'As
well as clearing the plates,' he continued with a chuckle.
The warm sound washed over her and she sighed out loud.
'I think today's been a good start.' Plus it had helped to
solidify his decision in allowing her to visit Spencer. The
fact that she was poring over toy catalogues, wanting to
find the perfect present for a little boy she didn't even
know, gave him some indication that she did have Spencer's best interests at heart.

Jane smiled shyly, bring her hair forward to hide her
face a little. The action on some women might look coy
and practised, but on Jane it only made her appear more
genuine. 'So do I,' she told him.

'Jane, I want you to meet Spencer. I want him to get to
know you and for you to spend time with him.' For what
seemed like an eternity Jane didn't say a word, only stared
at him across the table.

Finally, she managed to clear her throat and ask, 'Are

you sure?' She needed to check, needed to make sure because she'd been let down too many times in the past. She had to double-check before she allowed her elation to burst forth. 'I don't want you to think I'm pressuring you into this.'

Sean closed his eyes for a second, trying not to be disappointed that she hadn't instantly exploded with happiness, hugging him and smiling brightly up at him with those rich, green eyes of hers.

'That's not the case, Jane. I really do want you to know your nephew. Family is important. I understand that. Spencer *is* your family so it shouldn't matter whether we're friends or colleagues or...whatever.'

Whatever? Jane wondered what he might mean by that comment. Whatever?

'Jane?'

'Huh?' She blinked quickly, clearing her wayward thoughts. 'Sorry. You were saying?'

'I was saying I think it's only right for you to have access to Spencer.'

'And you're really sure?'

Jane stared at him for a moment, his words slowly sinking in. Sean was going to allow her to get to know Spencer! It was as though all her dreams had come true. Slowly, very slowly, she allowed her emotions to shine out.

'That's...' She sighed with relief as the smile continued to spread over her face. 'That's very good news. Thank you, Sean. *Thank you.*'

Sean stared at her, unable to believe the utter delight reflected on her face. He'd wanted to see a bright beaming smile and she was definitely giving him one. He'd wanted her eyes to twinkle with delight and that's exactly what was happening. But what he hadn't counted on was the way the two combined would make her look so incredibly beautiful, it momentarily robbed him of breath.

Inner beauty, he'd learned, was far more important than external beauty. Daina had been a knockout on the outside and broken on the inside. Not that he was comparing the sisters, but to say Jane's natural radiance was presently knocking him off balance was an understatement.

The other thing he hadn't counted on was the fact that, a moment later, she seemed to be struggling to keep tears at bay. She bit her lower lip, her cheeks becoming tinged with pink as she tried to suppress her emotions. 'Thank you, Sean,' she whispered, and this time he heard the pure gratitude in her voice. She clutched her hands together at her chest. 'I don't think I've ever been this happy.'

'Really?' He was astonished by the statement but didn't pursue it. Something so simple had made her happy?

'And you won't change your mind?'

Sean couldn't help the tingling of annoyance he felt at her question and was about to tell her that he was a man of his word and that she could rely on what he said when he remembered she'd endured years of Daina's behaviour. One minute nice, the next horrible. Perhaps Jane wasn't questioning *him* but rather seeking reassurance because she'd been let down too many times in the past.

Sean reached over and took her hand in his, noticing she gasped a little at the action, her green eyes flashing with something…was it repressed desire or just surprise? He hoped it was the former because ever since he'd met her he'd had a difficult time removing her from his thoughts. 'Jane.' His tone was slightly husky and he quickly cleared his throat. 'I promise that I'll always try to be open and honest with you—I think it's what we both need after the way we've been hurt in the past.'

'Uh-huh,' she agreed, completely mesmerised, not only

by his touch but by the way his gaze seemed to see right into her heart, stripping her of all her defences, leaving her naked and vulnerable before him.

Was that a good thing?

'All finished here?' the waiter asked, as he came over to clear their plates.

'Oh.' Jane quickly jerked her hand out of Sean's grasp and looked down at her empty plate and cup. 'Uh…yes. Yes. Thank you.'

Had she just been staring across a table into Sean's eyes, holding his hand…in public? This place was so close to the hospital that anyone could have walked in and seen them together and not have understood that it was all quite innocent and that nothing was going on between them except for the fact that he was granting her wish, that he was allowing her to see—

'Jane?'

'Hmm? Huh? What?' She looked across at him to find him smiling brightly at her, as though he could see the redness she could feel staining her cheeks. She looked away, dipping her head, using her hair as a shield against her embarrassment.

'When would you like to see Spencer?'

Jane wiped her face with her napkin before picking up the toy catalogue from the table as the waiter cleared everything away. She thanked him then opened her purse to get out some money. Sean quickly held up a hand to stop her.

'It's fine. I have an account here.'

'You do? You eat here that often?'

Sean nodded, instructing the waiter to put the food and drinks on his account. 'The food is made fresh and it's healthy. Besides, Ronan's daughter goes to school with Spencer so why not eat at a place you can trust?'

'Why not indeed,' she said. 'Well…then, thank you for lunch, Sean.'

'You sound surprised,' he remarked as he stood and came around the table to hold her chair for her.

'Thank you again,' she murmured, wishing he wouldn't be so chivalrous and gorgeous smelling and close and warm and inviting. It stalled the logical thought processes in her mind.

'You're welcome.' His smile was smooth, teasing and a little inviting, and Jane quickly picked up her bag and the catalogue and started for the door. She remembered to thank Ronan and his staff and to compliment the chef before she headed out of the cool air-conditioning into the heat.

'What time's the meeting about Tessa?' Sean asked, swatting away a fly.

'Not for another hour.'

'OK.' He nodded. 'Then, if you're not needed at the hospital, what would you like to do?'

Jane stared at him, surprised he hadn't simply made an excuse to leave. Did he *want* to spend more time with her? 'We could go to the toy store.' She held up the catalogue. 'Take a look around, see if there's anything there Spencer might like.'

'Great. Mind if I tag along?'

'You really want to?'

'He is my son after all, so I'll definitely be able to give you some pointers as to what he might like.'

Jane's smile was bright and her eyes twinkled. 'OK, then.'

'Every year you send him the most wonderful presents. He loves them.'

'He does?' She hadn't been sure whether Sean was passing on the gifts or whether he preferred Spencer not to have any contact whatsoever with her.

'It must be difficult, buying for someone you don't know.'

Jane shrugged. 'I just buy him what I wanted when I was his age. I know we're different genders but I was never really girly.' She'd left that to Daina. 'I loved cars and model aircraft and chemistry sets. Boys always have the better toys, as far as I'm concerned.'

'Well, you've always picked winners.'

'Wow. Yay, me!'

That gorgeous beaming smile was back and Sean drank it in. To say Jane was captivating him more and more with each passing second he spent in her company was an understatement.

'You're always so good with remembering his birthday,' Sean said. 'Never once have you forgotten.'

'It's a bit hard to forget Spencer's birthday.'

'Why?'

'Because it's the same day as mine. We share a birthday.' Jane delivered the line as though she was telling him the weather.

'You—? Wait. Spencer was born on your birthday?'

'He was.' Jane smiled up at him. 'That's why I've always felt such a strong connection with him. He's my birthday buddy. He'll turn seven and I'll turn thirty.'

Sean shook his head in astonishment. 'I had no idea. Daina…she never—' He stopped, both of them still strolling along. Jane looked up at him.

'She never talked about me, right?'

'Not really.'

'And I'll bet when she did it was usually derogatory in some way.'

'In the beginning, well, I guess I took everything she said as gospel.'

'But after that?'

'Do you mean when I realised my wife had serious mental health issues?' They stopped at a set of traffic lights and Sean pressed the button, both of them waiting for the lights to change. Jane turned to face him.

'How long did it take for you to realise?'

'About twelve months, I'm sorry to say. You'd think as a doctor I'd have picked up the signs and symptoms sooner.'

'You were no doubt very busy at the hospital, working all hours, and, believe me, Daina could be quite convincing when it suited her.'

Sean nodded. 'You sound as though you know exactly how I felt.'

'Let me guess. Whenever you tried to question her about things, she'd tell you that you were overreacting or that you'd grasped the wrong end of the stick. She'd give you just enough attention, indicating she understood what was happening, then she'd expertly turn the tables so that you were the one in the wrong, making you feel guilty and filled with remorse.'

'Yes.' Sean was astounded at just how well Jane articulated what he'd experienced, living with Daina.

'It's very difficult when you're emotionally involved with someone, when you love them, to realise they're manipulating you.'

'Yes.' He nodded slowly and exhaled. 'It wasn't until Daina started trying to turn me against my parents and siblings that I began to realise there wasn't something wrong with *me*, it was *her.*' He spread his hands wide. 'I knew what she'd said about my sisters couldn't possibly be true. I know them so well, we're a very close-knit family and when I discussed things openly with my sisters…well, it was then the blinkers finally came off.'

'But you were still married to her for almost six years, Sean.'

'She was my wife, Jane. She was mentally ill. I couldn't just abandon her.'

'I doubt she felt the same way about you.' The words were out of Jane's mouth before she could stop them and as the pedestrian light finally turned green she set off across the road. 'I'm sorry if that sounds harsh,' she continued as they started walking down the other side of the street, 'but I know Daina. I know the way she could manipulate and twist the situation and I know that even if you loved her, even if you tried to get her help, she would have done little to actually help herself.'

Jane glanced across at him, hoping she hadn't over-stepped the mark of this new level of friendship they seemed to be building. 'I'm sorry if what I've said of-fends you but—'

'No. You're absolutely right,' he interjected. 'But I've been raised to appreciate the value of family and, as my wife, Daina was my family. I wouldn't have been able to live with myself if I hadn't done everything I could to help her.'

'What did you try?' Jane asked as they neared the toy store.

'I organised appointments for her with mental health specialists. The first few times she refused to turn up and would often disappear for days or even weeks, not coming home and worrying me to the point of despair.'

'Yeah.' Her words were soft and she stopped under the shade of a nearby tree and looked up at Sean, who stood with his hands shoved into his pockets, his face drawn with remembered pain. 'Hiding from the truth.'

'A few times, though, I did manage to get her admitted to a clinic where she stayed for a few weeks, receiving medication for her condition, and it looked as though it was working.'

'But the instant she was discharged, after convincing everyone that she really was fine, things would begin to change again?'

'Yes.' Sean raked one hand through his hair. 'I tried everything I could to get her help but her problems, and she received so many diagnoses over the years, weren't easy to overcome if she wasn't willing to help herself.'

'Instead, everyone around the person suffers.'

Sean looked at Jane with concern as she spoke. She was looking down at the ground and when he reached out, lifting her chin so he could see her eyes, he saw pain reflected there. 'She hurt you a lot, didn't she?' It was a statement more than a question but Jane shrugged one shoulder, stepping back from his touch. Sean dropped his hand back to his side and watched her for another moment, seeing the years of unhappiness Jane had probably endured at the hands of her sister.

'So what finally ended it? You've already told me you were divorced before Daina passed away. What was it that made you end that toxic relationship?'

'Toxic. That's a good word for it.' Sean shoved both hands into his trouser pockets again and shifted his feet. 'She was pregnant with Spencer and at first she kept telling me how delighted she was, how this baby would change everything, make everything better between us, but it was just another one of her lies.'

Jane remained silent, watching the different array of emotions cross his face. Confusion, hurt, dejection, anger.

'I came home one day to find her gone. Usually when she left, or ran away, she'd pack a bag but this time nothing was missing. I checked the usual places, the different friends she relied on, but none of them knew where she was. Then two weeks later she came back home and seemed to be all right. She said she'd been confused, that she wanted to have the baby and that she loved me.'

Jane sighed. 'I know where she went during that time, Sean.'

'You do?'

She nodded. 'Daina came to see me. I was living in Melbourne and she'd somehow found me and turned up on my doorstep, saying she needed a place to stay for the night. As usually happened when Daina was around, all she talked about was herself, that to start off with she'd thought she'd wanted a baby, that it might be fun, but that she'd been in the shopping centre where a baby had been crying. Constantly crying, not stopping, and she realised she didn't want a baby after all. She said she'd tried to get an abortion but she was too far along with the pregnancy. The abortion clinics had turned her away.' Jane sighed heavily. 'That was why she'd come to see me.'

Sean gulped. 'She wanted you to do an abortion!'

'Yes.'

'What did you say?'

'That she was a fool. That she was too selfish to see that she had it all. She had good looks, a loving husband and was now going to have a child. I told her I was jealous of her. That seemed to feed her ego enough and she started talking about keeping the baby. It was all I could think of to ensure she didn't do something else to try and terminate the pregnancy.'

'How many weeks gestation was she?'

'Thirty-one.'

'What happened after that?'

'She left, telling me she was going to return home to

her wonderful life with her loving husband. I hoped it was the truth.'

'And at thirty-three weeks I returned from a late shift at the hospital to discover her lying at the bottom of the stairs.'

'Oh, no.'

'She was drifting in and out of consciousness and she was cold. She'd sustained a concussion and at one point it did look as though she might lose the baby.'

'Obviously, Spencer managed to pull through.'

At the mention of his son, Sean smiled. 'He's a tough little lad. Resilient.' The smile slowly faded as he met Jane's gaze. 'After his birth, Daina admitted to me that she hadn't accidentally fallen down the stairs as I'd presumed.'

Jane gasped, covering her mouth as she whispered, 'She'd thrown herself down voluntarily.'

He nodded. 'Yes.'

'What happened?'

'I finally saw the real Daina. After almost six years of my life, during which I'd tried everything I could to make her happy, to give her what she wanted, to try and please her, I saw her true self. She admitted that she'd continued drinking and even taking drugs throughout the pregnancy in the hope that the baby would abort spontaneously, but it hadn't so, in her mind, terminating the pregnancy herself was the next logical conclusion.'

'She always had such a convoluted way of thinking.'

'Yes.' He looked at Jane. 'You understand completely.' He reached out and took her hand in his. Jane tried not to react to the warmth that shot up her arm and burst into a mass of tingles throughout her entire body. Why on earth did one simple touch from him affect her in such a way?

'I've never been able to talk to anyone else about Daina,' he continued, completely unaware of how she was feeling.

She wanted to pull her hand away but knew that would raise more questions than anything else. Instead, she focused on what he was saying. 'Not even my parents, as close as we are, really grasped the full level of Daina's vindictiveness. Sure, they could see she was a little unstable at times but she was quite the actress and played us all.'

'Yes.' Jane shifted back a little, the action causing Sean to casually release her hand. She quickly grasped the toy catalogue from her bag, needing something to hold onto, trying desperately to concentrate on what he was saying rather than the way he was making her feel.

Even her own parents hadn't understood the full extent of Daina's moods, hadn't seen the way she'd emotionally bullied Jane for years prior to the accident. Now, with Sean, Jane was finally coming to realise, just as he was, that someone else *truly* understood. It provided them with an instant bond, even though it was formed through negative experiences.

'Spencer,' Sean continued, 'was in the neonate intensive care unit for the next three months but he was a fighter. After the delivery Daina was kept in overnight for observation and was then discharged, but before she left the hospital I told her our marriage was over. I would be filing for divorce as soon as possible and that if she didn't agree, if she did anything to contest it, I would have her charged with attempted manslaughter of our child.'

'You were angry.'

'I was livid, not only at her but at myself. I couldn't believe I'd been such a fool and for such a long time.'

'You made up rational excuses for her behaviour,' Jane offered.

'Exactly.' He spread his arms wide. 'I can't believe how…freeing it is to talk to you like this, Jane. You understand.'

'I do.'

Sean paused for a moment, looking at her as though he was seeing her for the time. She was not merely Daina's sister or Spencer's aunt...she was Jane, a woman who had clearly been through some terrible emotional experiences but instead of allowing them to make her weak had drawn strength from them, working hard and specialising in treating children with eating disorders who were also lost. She was trying to make a difference in the world and that realisation made him appreciate her even more.

CHAPTER FIVE

'WELL,' SEAN SAID after a long moment. They'd stood there, staring at each other, and Jane found herself becoming a little self-conscious, especially as Sean seemed to be looking at her as though he'd just discovered a rare treasure. Surely that couldn't be right. Jane had never classified herself as a rare anything. 'We have to do something,' he continued as he started walking again.

'For what?'

'For your birthday,' he stated, as though it was completely obvious.

Jane realised he was changing the subject and she was more than happy for that to occur. Still, the thought of having someone actually plan something for her birthday was more than she could contemplate right now. 'Oh, no. It's fine.' She brushed his words away. 'Focusing on Spencer is better. You only turn seven once and it's a big deal in a boy's life...or so I've gathered from my young patients over the years.'

For some reason he felt a strange sense of responsibility for Jane's happiness. Although Daina had torn his life to shreds, he'd had the support of his parents and siblings to help him through, especially where Spencer was concerned. Jane had had no one. If he didn't do something for her birthday, who would? Sean decided it would be best not to pursue the matter at the moment but he also made a note to ensure that this year Jane would have a birthday she wouldn't forget.

'So when would you like to meet Spencer?' Sean asked, as they continued down the street towards the toy store.

'I was going to leave that up to you. I don't want Spencer to be all nervous and worried about meeting a new aunty. I don't want it to be a "Surprise! You have a new relative" sort of thing.'

Sean laughed at her words. 'It wouldn't be like that. He knows he has an Aunt Jane, he's seen a picture of you—'

'Really? You have a picture of me?'

'I believe you were in a few that were taken at the funeral.'

'Oh.'

'Spencer's not completely in the dark about your existence.'

'Good to know…and thank you, Sean.'

'For?'

'For telling him about me. For not allowing me to be overlooked, even though things didn't work out with Daina.' Her words were filled with gratitude. As he held the door for her to enter the toy store, he thought it odd. Of course he wasn't going to hide her existence from his son. That would not only be dishonest but also cruel. Why would Jane even think he'd do—?

He stopped his thoughts. Daina. She'd said some terrible things to him about Jane, so no doubt she'd said some terrible things about him to Jane. Jane had grown up in the shadow of her very pretty, very dominant big sister and he had the distinct feeling that she'd been overlooked more than once during her childhood.

It made him want to introduce her to Spencer this afternoon but perhaps she was right and that he should at least prime his son first, even though he knew Spencer would do nothing except accept the situation his father presented. He was a very well-adjusted boy and if his father said it was OK, then it would be OK. The knowledge filled Sean's heart with paternal pride.

As he watched Jane walk around the toy store, picking up things here and there, he quickly went through the rest of his weekly schedule in his mind.

'How about Friday afternoon?' he said as he came up behind Jane, who was looking at a remote-controlled dinosaur and giggling.

'Friday afternoon? To meet Spencer?' She gulped. 'That's in…two days' time.'

'Well, I was going to suggest this afternoon but I know you have meetings so it wouldn't work out.'

'This afternoon?' She gulped and stared at him with wide eyes.

'But then I thought that perhaps both of you might need to get used to the idea.'

'I would do it,' she said quickly, in case he thought she was backing out. 'I would come this afternoon. Don't think I wouldn't. It's just that I've thought about this and wanted this for so long that to actually have a dream come true and—'

Sean chuckled and reached out to put a hand on Jane's shoulder. 'It's fine, Jane. I understand you need a bit of time to mentally prepare yourself. So…Friday? You can come with me to pick him up from his drum lesson.'

'He plays the drums?' Jane's earlier panic disappeared and she smiled brightly. 'I've always wanted to learn.'

'Perhaps he can teach you a thing or two although at the moment it's more a matter of him trying to gain some upper-body strength in his little almost-seven-year-old arms.' Sean laughed.

'That's fantastic. I'd love to hear him play.'

'Oh, you'll get the chance. One basic beat after the other. He loves to practise, although I'm not sure my parents or the rest of the neighbourhood are all that happy about it.'

'Your parents?'

'They live with us.'

'They do?'

Sean nodded as they continued to browse around the toy store. 'It's the only way I can work at the hospital, be available at all hours of the day and night and still give Spencer the relatively normal upbringing he deserves. We converted a house into two apartments. One upstairs, one downstairs.'

'Sounds ideal. What time does his drum lesson finish?'

'Five-thirty. You don't have a car, do you?'

'No.'

'OK. We both have clinic on Friday afternoon so, once we're finished, I'll take you to meet my son.'

Sean nodded with finality as though the deal was done. Jane swallowed as the realisation sank in. She was going to meet Spencer. It was happening. Things were working out as planned, instead of going pear-shaped, like they usually did, especially when it came to her private life. Spencer. She'd loved him ever since she'd been aware of him and now she was finally going to meet him…in two days' time!

Should she get him a present for when they first met? A sort of a 'Hello. How are you?' present? Was that crass? Perhaps she should buy some sweets or take some cake but she had no idea if Spencer had any food allergies. What about a book? Should she get him a book? Her mind went into overdrive as she walked around the store, settling in front of the music section and looking at all the different types of drumsticks available.

'I should get him a present for Friday,' she stated, taking a pair of drumsticks off the shelf.

'He doesn't need presents, Jane. He's already spoilt enough.' Sean took the sticks from her and put them back, before meeting her gaze. 'Your presence will be present enough.'

His words were soft yet intense and the way he stared at her made her wonder if he, too, could feel this strange and overwhelming tug of desire that seemed to exist between them. How? Why? She didn't understand how it was possible for her to be so attracted to Sean. The man had been married to her sister and—

No. That was in the past. The past couldn't be changed. The past was irrelevant. She'd trained her mental thought processes to stop looking back, to seek out the future but also not to miss the present…and at the present moment she couldn't deny the way Sean's intense gaze was making her feel.

She needed to say something to break the moment, to try and remember how to breathe again. 'OK,' she murmured, and forced herself to blink, to turn away and head to the rear of the store, where a model train was presently manoeuvring its way around the track.

Jane stopped, staring at a doll on the shelf in the back corner of the store. She frowned as memories flooded through, unbidden. A moment later Sean joined her and casually pointed to the doll.

'Now I know you like to buy Spencer different presents for his birthday but I know for a fact that dolls just aren't his thing.'

'I used to have one of these.' Jane reached out her hand, belatedly realising she was trembling a little, and picked up the boxed doll. 'If you pressed her belly button and gently pulled on the hair, the hair would grow. At the back, there was a winder to crank the hair back inside.' Jane trailed her fingers down the plastic packaging of the box. 'Mine was called Cinnamon.'

'You don't still have the doll?'

'No.' Jane sighed. 'Daina had one of her tantrums—I can't remember what it was all about—only that she was so mad she punished me by cutting off all of Cinnamon's hair so it didn't grow or shrink any more. I was upset but I could still play with the doll. However, a few weeks later, when she realised I hadn't abandoned the wrecked doll, she took it and hid it. I looked everywhere and then three weeks after Cinnamon had gone missing I found the doll all over my bedroom floor, in pieces.'

'How old were you?' Sean had listened to the way she'd spoken, so calm and controlled, as though she was reliving the memory of someone else.

'Eight.'

'What did your parents say?'

Jane slowly shook her head. 'They didn't know. I learned at a very early age that if I attempted to involve my parents when Daina acted out, the retribution was ten times worse.'

'She hit you?'

'No. She never laid a finger on me. She had other ways of making my life miserable.' Jane put the doll back on the shelf then walked away.

They continued to look around the store until Jane picked up a little torch that had small covers you could put over the light, causing it to make different shapes on the wall. Without a word, she headed to the register to make her purchase, asking them to gift wrap it for her.

'I'd best head back to the hospital. There are some case studies I'd like to read before the meeting about Tessa.'

'Of course.' They walked back to the hospital, both

lost in their own thoughts but also quite comfortable with the silence. It was odd to feel so comfortable with Sean but perhaps, now that she had an answer to her question, now that she'd been granted access to Spencer, the previous tension she'd felt between the two of them had disappeared. No. Not disappeared…changed. She pushed the thought away, knowing she'd give it due consideration later when he wasn't affecting her senses as much as he was doing now.

'Regarding Tessa,' Sean said after a while, swatting away another fly as they drew closer to the hospital, 'she's being abused, isn't she?'

'There's always a reason why kids don't eat and it's usually the biggest cry for help they can give us doctors. Besides, there are many different forms of abuse. It's just figuring out which one.'

'You obviously have an idea what might be happening.'

'I have a theory but I don't want to say anything until there's further proof.'

'Gut instinct?'

'Uh-huh.'

'It's good to know you follow your instincts. It can be a doctor's most valuable tool.'

'I'm glad to hear you think that way,' she said, turning to smile up at him. Again, Sean was struck by how lovely she was, how real, how natural.

When they entered the building, they both sighed with relief at being surrounded by the air-conditioning. Jane headed to the ward and found the medical students seated at the nurses' station, the notepads in front of them filled with different observations and notes. Jane stopped and spoke with them for a moment before she went over to where Tessa was sitting up in her bed, reading a book.

Sean stayed where he was, watching closely as Tessa's

expression seemed to soften when she saw Jane. He'd never noticed Tessa do that with anyone else. He checked the notes the nurses had written, noticing that Tessa hadn't eaten anything all day but, thankfully, hadn't made any attempt to pull out her drip, as she had once before.

There was a gasp of surprise and he looked over to see Tessa's big eyes widen as she opened the present from Jane. Within another minute she'd flicked the torch on and off several times, discovering that if she turned the rim, the light would change colour. She put the different covers over the bulb, testing each one, clearly enthralled with the gift. Then she put it down on the bedside table and shook her head. Sean edged closer, wanting to hear what Jane was saying to the girl.

'There are no strings attached,' she told Tessa softly. 'I know what it's like to accept a gift from someone who later demands payment—often a payment that's too high for you to give.'

Tessa watched Jane for a moment then asked, 'Who hurt you?'

The colour instantly drained from Jane's face and Sean watched as she bit her lip and swallowed three times before answering. 'My big sister.'

'Where is she now?'

'She died.'

'Did you kill her?'

'No. She was in a car crash.'

'I wish my sister was in a car crash.' The words were out of Tessa's mouth before she could stop them and she quickly covered her mouth with her hands, her eyes wide and wild with fear. 'Don't tell anyone. Don't say anything.' Her pleading was an urgent whisper.

Jane looked directly at Sean and it was only then he realised she'd known he was there the whole time. Had she just said all of that to Tessa in order to get the little girl to confess? To let them know exactly who was hurting her? This information would certainly help the medical students to hone their observation skills now they knew exactly what they were looking for.

'I'll come back and see you later tonight,' Jane promised, before pointing to the torch. 'There are no strings attached to this gift, Tessa. It's just something to help you not to be so afraid of the night.'

'How did you know it was her sister?' Sean asked Jane as they re-entered the nurses' station.

'I didn't, but sometimes sharing your own stories with these kids, to let them know you really do understand what they're going through, even though the circumstances of the abuse might differ, is an important step in forming a connection. I've chosen to utilise the bad things that have happened to me throughout my life in order to help me bond with my patients, because when eating disorders are involved, it's been proved through extensive research that if a true connection can be made between doctor and patient, there's far more opportunity for a successful recovery.'

'That must be very draining for you.'

Jane shrugged. 'It helps abate the loneliness.' She spoke to the medical students, asking them if Tessa's sister had come in to visit and to highlight those sections when they gave their report. 'I need to prepare for the meeting,' she murmured, and Sean nodded, still reeling from everything he'd learnt about her today.

As she walked away, he couldn't help thinking back to the things Daina had said about her younger sister. It wasn't that she'd talked about Jane or her parents much at all, but if she had had something to say, it had always shown *her* in the best light, to ensure he was left with a positive opinion of her.

'I took Jane in.' He could hear Daina's voice in his head. 'I was only eighteen when our parents died but I was there for Janey throughout her time in hospital and I cared for her, stepping up and being her legal guardian to ensure she wasn't put into the foster system. It wasn't easy. I was grieving for our parents and looking after a confused teenager who was terribly sick, both physically and mentally. It was tiring and exhausting but I managed, by the grace of God, to get us through that difficult time.' And of course every word Daina had spoken had been delivered with the dramatic flair of an award-winning actress, oftentimes with tears.

As he returned to his office to try and once more distract his mind with paperwork, he instead found himself looking Jane up on the internet. Surprisingly, he was able to access several of the papers she'd co-authored with Professor Robe and soon he was reading his way through them. He shook his head in stunned amazement. Jane was clearly an expert in her field, as well as being incredibly intelligent and sensitive. The hospital had been right to head-hunt and secure her professional services for twelve months.

Twelve months. She'd been here for one already. Eleven months of her getting to know Spencer, and of spending more time with her away from the hospital. Sean couldn't deny the delight he felt at that thought. He would brush away everything he could remember Daina saying about her sister and start afresh.

'A clean slate,' he told his cramped office. 'For both of us.'

CHAPTER SIX

THE MEETING ABOUT Tessa went well, with the medical students able to provide data about Tessa's behaviour when her parents came to visit, bringing her older and younger siblings with them.

'She was fine with the toddler,' one medical student reported. 'Pulling him onto her bed and hugging him close.'

'She wants to protect him,' Jane murmured. 'And the older sibling?'

'The older daughter, who is approximately nine or ten years of age, was almost...' The medical students looked at each other, both a little unsure.

'Go on,' Jane encouraged.

'Well, she wasn't mean at all. In fact, she was really nice to Tessa. She'd even brought Tessa in a present and was making Tessa laugh.'

Jane clenched her jaw and tried to keep her own feelings under control. 'Passive aggressive,' was all she said.

'But Tessa was laughing,' one of the students said, completely perplexed.

'No. Tessa was playing the part she needs to play in order to protect herself and her baby brother.' Jane looked at the data provided by the students. 'See here?' she said, pointing to an entry made half an hour after Tessa's family had left. 'She went to the toilet then went back to her bed, curling up small and almost hiding beneath the covers.'

'Do you think she was trying to vomit in the toilets?' Sean asked.

'Trying to purge herself of the way she was feeling? Yes. At the moment the drip is keeping her fluids up and the antibiotics are treating her urinary tract infection but the act of physically trying to purge the negative emotions is quite common in such cases.' Jane picked up the articles she'd photocopied and handed them around to the dietician, social worker and nurses also attending the meeting.

As Jane continued to point out different case studies, Sean listened with half an ear, admiring the way she understood not only the psychological but physical implications of what her patients were going through. Did that mean that Jane herself had suffered from an eating disorder as a young child? Had Daina's bullying caused Jane to try and purge the negative emotions from her body? Was that why she wore such loose-fitting clothing? Did she still suffer from an eating disorder?

Concern flooded through Sean as he watched her move. Her long hair swished down her back as she moved over to the white board and began breaking down Tessa's symptoms. The fact that Jane had also managed to prise a confession out of Tessa only served to corroborate the signs and symptoms.

'So what do we do?' Anthea asked. 'How can we help poor little Tessa?'

'Excellent question,' Jane replied, and for the first time since they'd entered the meeting she smiled. The action lit up her features and Sean was once more struck by her inner beauty. Did she have any idea just how beautiful she was?

For the rest of the meeting they formulated a plan of action to help Tessa, as well as getting some help for the older sibling. Had the parents noticed anything? Were they also afraid of their oldest daughter, unable to impose any parental control on her? It did happen. Jane had seen it with her own parents. Oftentimes they'd found it much easier to placate Daina than stand their ground. She hoped that with this early intervention for Tessa the situation would be defined and coping strategies put in place for all concerned.

After the meeting Jane couldn't believe how drained she felt and so she slipped away quietly, not bothering to say goodbye to anyone. Back in the residential wing, she put her phone and hospital lanyard onto the table beside the bed and kicked off her shoes. She lay down on the bed and allowed the cool air-conditioning to soothe her.

No sooner had she closed her eyes than her phone rang. 'Not happening,' she moaned, as she reached out to pick up her cell and answer it. 'Dr Diamond,' she said, trying to hide the tiredness in her voice.

'Jane? Where are you?'

'Sean? I'm in my room. In the res wing.'

'You're OK.'

'Of course I'm OK. Why wouldn't I be?'

'Well, you just disappeared.' There was a hint of annoyance as well as relief in his tone. 'I would have walked you over to the res wing. Although it's in hospital grounds, that doesn't mean it's one hundred per cent safe. I was worried.'

'You were worried?' Her eyebrows hit her hairline.

'Of course I was.'

'About me?' she asked, disbelief lacing her words.

'Look, Jane. I know you haven't had a normal upbringing so this may come as a shock to you, but families look after each other, care for each other. I may have driven my twin sisters crazy with my over-protective big-brother routine while we were growing up but they also knew it was only because I cared.'

'You…care?' Her words were hesitant.

'About you? Yes. You're Spencer's aunty. So are my sisters and, as such, you deserve the same consideration as them.'

Jane tried to process his words, still unsure what this 'consideration' might entail. Did that mean Sean saw her in the role of a surrogate sister? Had she misinterpreted those long, lingering looks they'd shared?

'Oh. Well, I apologise for not saying goodbye. I was tired and I'm not really used to having people…care about me in that way. You know, concerned for my safety and all that.'

'Well, you'd better start getting used to it. Family is family and I'm very protective of mine.'

'As you should be.'

'That now includes you, Jane.'

'It does?'

'Yes!' The word was filled with exasperation and Jane couldn't help but smile. Sean cared about her? He considered her as part of his family, even though she hadn't even met Spencer yet? The sensation of being so accepted overwhelmed her and she pursed her lips together in an effort to stop the tears of happiness she could feel welling up inside her. Sean cared.

'I've never had anyone, protective or otherwise, really care, so you'll have to forgive me if I don't follow protocol.'

'That's all right,' he said, his tone more calm. Sean leaned back in his chair and put his feet up on the desk. 'I'll guide you through any rocky waters.' He smiled as he spoke. Jane had such a soothing voice, sweet, calm and controlled. He'd seen those gorgeous green eyes of hers flashing with anger or glowing with complete happiness, but how would she look, how would she sound when she was filled with desire?

He closed his eyes on the thought and immediately pushed it away. He shouldn't be thinking about her in such a way and yet he didn't seem able to stop himself. All those years ago when he'd met Daina, things had moved incredibly fast and he'd been married before he'd known which way was up. He knew now that that had just been Daina's style, but with Jane he had the sense that a slowly-slowly approach would no doubt benefit both of them.

He'd only started to really get to know her a few days ago but what he was seeing, the inner character she was revealing, was…breathtaking. He was beginning to realise just how much she'd missed out on, not only during her childhood but also as an adult. She'd been so incredibly lonely that she'd risked moving to Adelaide. She'd put her heart on the line, almost begging him to allow her access to Spencer. How could any man not be affected by her genuine heart? How could he not want to wrap his arms about her and protect her from any future hurts?

'Any big dinner plans for tonight?' he found himself asking, imagining arriving at her door with take-out, the two of them eating and chatting amicably together in her small, intimate room.

'Toast and jam.' Her answer was accompanied by a big yawn and the image in Sean's head evaporated. She was tired, exhausted.

'Do you have trouble sleeping?'

'Sometimes. It's another reason why I'm more than happy to stay here, close to the hospital. If I can't sleep, at least I can catch up on some work or check on my patients.'

'Or sing to them.'

'Or that.' She chuckled.

'You have a lovely voice. Soothing. Relaxing.'

'Well, any time you're stressed, give me a call and I'll sing you a lullaby.'

'I'm stressed right now.' The words were out of his mouth before he could stop them. Why had he said that? To hear Jane's pretty singing voice coming down the line would only serve to intensify the emotions he was attempting to keep under control. Before he could say anything else, Jane immediately began to sing.

Her lilting voice surrounded him and he leaned back further in his chair, letting the lyrics and melody blend together. He could feel the tensions of his day begin to disappear, his breathing deepening as he completely filled his lungs with oxygen before inhaling slowly.

At the end of the first verse and chorus, Jane stopped to yawn and he couldn't help but laugh. 'You're de-stressing yourself as well.'

'I think you might be right.' She yawned again. 'I think I'd best say goodnight before I fall asleep with the phone glued to my ear.'

'Wise move.' He chuckled. 'Goodnight, Jane. Sleep sweet,' he murmured, before disconnecting the call, *and* before he gave in to the urge to rush to the res wing and haul her into his arms. How could one short song make him feel as though he'd just found the most perfect place to call home? He didn't need any new complications in his life, especially as he'd worked hard since Spencer's birth to maintain a certain level of detachment from romantic relationships. He'd tried dating once or twice but with the distrust Daina's antics had instilled deep within him he had become naturally suspicious of the most innocent actions.

So why didn't he feel that way with Jane? How could he be absolutely certain she was as genuine as she appeared? He frowned, not wanting to listen to the doubting voice. 'Meeting Spencer will be the true test,' he said, as he took his feet off the desk and stood. Spencer had a good intuitive sense about him, most children did because they weren't as fooled by deception as adults could be.

As he collected the papers he needed to work on and locked up his office, Sean found himself wishing it was Friday afternoon already. Seeing Jane face to face with his son would help give him the reassurance he was looking for.

After clinic on Friday afternoon, Jane couldn't believe how jittery she felt.

'I'm as nervous as a long-tailed cat in a room full of rocking chairs,' she told Sean, as she finished writing up the last set of casenotes.

'You'll do fine.' He checked his watch. 'We have a good half an hour before we need to pick Spencer up.'

'Really?' She checked the time on her cellphone. 'We finished clinic on time? How miraculous.' Sean chuckled at her words and she felt a wash of tingles spread down her spine at the sound. She'd made him laugh and the thought filled her with a bit more confidence about the important meeting awaiting her.

'Do you think I have time to change?' She stood. 'If you bring your car around to the res wing car park, I could meet you there.'

'Sure, but for the record you look lovely just as you are.'

Jane stared down at her long, ankle-length skirt, flat shoes and baggy shirt, her hair pulled out of the way in a loopy sort of ponytail. 'I do?'

'Yes.' His smile was genuine as he realised she truly had no idea just how lovely she was. He wanted to ask her if she wore the baggy clothes because she was self-conscious about her body. He wanted to know if she'd had an eating disorder as a child. She didn't seem to be suffering from it now but what would he know? Apart from having lunch with her the other day, he hadn't seen her eat much. He brushed the thoughts aside for now. 'OK, you head over to the res wing and I'll meet you there.'

It didn't take him long to move his car from one car park to the next and he headed inside the residential wing's lobby, sitting down in the cool air-conditioning and taking the opportunity to read the latest hospital news circular. No sooner had he started reading the lead article than he realised Jane was standing in front of him. He put the circular down and slowly stood up, his gaze travelling over the woman before him.

Dressed in jeans, flat shoes and a long-sleeved T-shirt that was still a little big for her, there was no doubting that she had a beautiful feminine shape. Add to that the fact that she'd plaited her long luscious locks into pigtails, making her look more like the seventeen-year-old he remembered, and Sean's previous warnings to himself to take things slowly seemed to disappear.

When she shoved her glasses onto her nose, a move he was coming to realise indicated she was nervous, he belatedly realised he'd been staring at her.

'Er...sorry.' Sean cleared his throat and thrust his hands into his pockets.

'Is this OK? Not too casual? I wasn't sure how formal or informal I should be.'

Sean smiled. 'Just be yourself and, if I might say so, you look lovely.'

'Lovely?'

'Yes, Jane.'

She lowered her head again but not before he'd seen the disbelief reflected in her eyes. 'How can you not know how beautiful you are?' he asked softly, stepping a little closer to her so others in the lobby didn't overhear what he was saying. 'Your hair is...glorious. When it's loose, I want to touch it, to watch as the silky strands slide through my fingers. And your eyes…' He exhaled slowly as he looked deeply into her eyes. 'So sad and intense. A man could lose himself in your eyes.'

'Uh…' Jane stumbled, breaking her gaze from his and looking down at the floor, feeling completely out of her depth. No one had ever spoken to her like this before, not even Eamon. Why was he saying these things to her?

'You're caring, intelligent and have the voice of an angel.' Sean reached out, placing his fingers gently beneath her chin, lifting her head so their eyes could meet once more. 'You're a person of worth, Jane Diamond. Far too many people have told you otherwise and it's time for that to change. You are a person of worth,' he repeated. 'And I for one am proud to call you my friend.'

'Friend,' she whispered, as though she were just learning to speak a new language. 'You're right, Sean.' She swallowed over the dryness in her throat. 'No one's ever told me that. Thank you.'

As she stared up at him, he knew what he'd said was completely true as her green eyes seemed to be inviting him to stare into them for ever. Such an odd sensation and one he was all too tempted by. However, the last thing either of them needed right now was any sort of romantic attachment. Logically, he accepted that. Emotionally, he didn't seem able to stop thinking about her.

Tonight he should be focused on keeping her calm, helping her through the apprehension he could already see was buzzing through her. He dropped his hand and took a step back, before forcing a smile. He held his hand out towards the door. 'We don't want to keep Spencer waiting. Shall we?'

Jane nodded, as though she were no longer capable of speech. Thankfully, his car wasn't too far from the entrance to the res wing so they were effectively going from one cooled place to another. Neither of them spoke for a while as Sean navigated the evening traffic, but once they were away from the hospital he glanced over at her.

She was tense. Both hands clenched tightly together in her lap. Her gaze was directly ahead, watching the traffic. Was she tense because she was in a car or was she nervous about the upcoming meeting? Sean decided it didn't really matter which one it was but tried his best to relax her a little.

'I read the last paper you published with Professor Robe.'

'Really?' She seemed surprised.

'Yes. It was very interesting as well as thorough but there are a few things I'm still not one hundred per cent sure about. You mentioned in the article the initial methodology required further investigation before you were able to employ the present model.'

'That's right.' There was a stronger note in her words, as though her mind was definitely shifting to more comfortable ground.

'What was the initial methodology you used?'

'Well...' And throughout the rest of the drive to the place where Spencer had his drum lesson, Sean kept asking questions and Jane kept answering them, her smooth voice combined with her intelligent words definitely assisted in focusing his train of thought, although once or twice when he stopped at red lights, he wasn't able to resist watching her mouth as she spoke. Such a perfectly shaped mouth as well.

'And here we are,' he said, as she just finished explaining the negative side effects of the medication doctors had previously used to treat urinary tract and bladder infections, which were common ailments associated with eating disorders.

'What? Here?' Jane looked at her surroundings, astonished. Then she looked back at Sean. 'You distracted me.' It was almost an accusation and Sean couldn't help but laugh. She looked so indignant it was adorable.

'It was clear you were over-thinking things and, besides, I really did want to know about your initial methodology.'

Jane slowly exited the car and looked over at him. 'Hmm. I guess I'll believe you.'

'Oh, thank you. Very much.'

There was a wonderful, natural smile on his face, such as she hadn't seen before. Combined with the delight in his eyes and the way his deep laughter vibrated through her, it was a wonder she could stand. Now, however, was not the time to be thinking about Sean or about the way his nearness affected her. She was here to meet Spencer.

Jane tried to calm her breathing. She'd looked forward to this day for so long...well, almost from the day Spencer was born. How she'd longed to be a part of his life and now, thanks to Sean, she was getting that opportunity.

'Coming?' Sean asked, and it was only then she realised he was walking up the path towards the house where loud drum beats could be heard. She slowly moved away from the car.

'Does he know I'm coming?'

'Yes. He's very interested to meet you.' He waved away her concerns as he pushed open the door and walked right in. 'You'll be fine,' he called, speaking a little louder over the drum beats.

To her surprise, the house they entered had a large practice room with a baby grand, a drum kit, keyboards and several other instruments set up, ready to play. But it was the boy sitting behind a set of drums that looked far too big for him, hammering out a steady beat in time to some rock music, who really caught her attention. The boy was a mini replica of his father, except that Spencer's hair was a little longer, curling slightly at the back.

Spencer finished playing the song, doing a drum-roll flourish at the end and hitting the cymbal loudly. Jane couldn't contain herself and let go of Sean's hand before she started clapping. Sean joined in and, in the next moment, Spencer's face lit up at the sight of his father.

'I'm so purple at it.' He held his drumsticks high in the air and they clapped louder. Jane beamed from ear to ear, unable to believe this moment had finally arrived.

'Purple?' she asked, momentarily looking towards Sean.

'It means brilliant.' He shrugged. 'Don't ask me more than that. Kids nowadays make up their own lingo and sometimes I think it's purely to keep us adults in the dark.'

Jane giggled, unable to believe how happy she felt, and she hadn't even spoken to Spencer yet. She didn't have long to wait as the boy wriggled out from behind the drum kit and raced over to his father.

'Dude.' Sean held up his hand and Spencer dutifully gave his father a high five. 'That was so purple.'

'I know, right!' Spencer grinned at his father then turned and looked at Jane, before angling his head to one side. 'Are you my new aunty? Aunty Jane?'

Jane pushed her glasses up the bridge of her nose and nodded. 'Yes. Yes, I am.'

'That's *totally* purple!' he yelled jovially, and within the next instant the young almost-seven-year-old had launched himself at her, wrapping his arms about her waist. Tears flooded into Jane's eyes as she put her hands on Spencer's back then looked over at the boy's father.

'It is. It's totally purple.' She laughed, happier than she could ever remember being.

CHAPTER SEVEN

THE HUG DIDN'T last long at all. In fact, it was over and done with as Spencer seemed to jump around the room, shifting from foot to foot as he told his father about his day. He kept looking at Jane, accepting her so instantly that her heart was overwhelmed with a pure love she'd never felt before.

After a moment he stopped still in his tracks, tipped his head to the side and looked at Jane intently. 'Hang on. You're the Aunty Jane who always sends me those cool presents for my birthday and Christmas, right?'

'That's right.'

'We did discuss this last night as well as this morning,' Sean gently reminded his son, but it appeared Spencer only had eyes for his new aunt at the moment.

'I love the microscope you sent for Christmas. Dad and I looked at a drop of blood on a slide and I wrote you a letter to say thank you but I didn't know where you lived so I didn't get to send it but now that you're here, I can give it to you.'

Jane's heart turned over with delight. 'I'd like that.'

'Super green. Did you want to come to my house?'

'Uh...yes. I'd like that very much. Thank you, Spencer.'

'Green,' he said with a nod. 'I've gotta pack up my stuff.' He took a step towards the drum kit then stopped and turned to look at her. 'Hey, because you're here and it's my birthday soon, does that mean I'm not gonna get a cool present?'

'Spencer!' Sean immediately chastised his son.

'It's all right, Sean. It's a fair question,' Jane interjected. 'Perhaps we can work something out. Perhaps we could go shopping together?'

'Really?' Spencer's eyes lit up.

'It means the present wouldn't be a surprise but you could definitely choose what you wanted.' And she'd get to spend time with him. 'If it's OK with your dad,' she added, looking at Sean. Although he was willing to give her access to Spencer, Jane still didn't want to overstep any boundaries. She needed to keep things on an even keel lest Sean retract his permission. Jane was very good at not rocking the boat, at realising where her boundaries were, but with Sean…when he was close to her, speaking in those deep and sensual tones, telling her she was lovely…when that happened, she had no idea where the boundaries were!

Being around Sean was unsettling but in a good way. He had definitely ignited a spark when he'd confessed he wanted to run his fingers through her hair. How was she supposed to take a comment like that? How was she supposed to keep things on an even keel so she could continue to see Spencer, when Sean continually knocked her completely off balance?

Spencer picked up his music books and put them into his bag. 'It'll be OK, won't it, Dad,' he stated with confidence. 'Aunty Jane and I can go shopping, can't we?' He looked pleadingly up at his father. 'And after the shops we can all go home and play with whatever I get and you and Dad can have a coffee.' Spencer slung his music bag over his shoulder, looping the bag across his body, and spread his hands wide, as though everything seemed organised and perfectly normal.

Jane was still holding onto the way the words 'Aunty Jane' had rolled so easily off his tongue. Oh, to be so innocent, to be so secure in parental love. It was clear, even after just a few minutes of meeting Spencer, that Sean had done a wonderful job of raising his son.

'I love meeting new aunties,' he remarked with an air of superiority, as though he had relatives popping out of the woodwork every single day of the week. 'I already have two aunties, two uncles and three cousins and two grandparents and Dad, and now I have *another* aunty. This is so purple.'

Spencer waved goodbye to his music teacher, remembering to thank him for the lesson before his father scolded him for having bad manners, then headed to the door.

'Are you all right?' Sean asked softly. Jane had been unaware he'd moved to stand beside her, the warmth emanating from him surrounding her like a comfortable, snuggly blanket, safe and secure. She blinked and smiled, then laughed through the blend of emotions. Happiness, joy, confusion, acceptance, awareness. It was all too much for her so, instead of trying to figure things out, as she usually did, she was simply going to accept that this was the way she felt and there was nothing else to do except go with it.

'I'm purple and super green and all the other colours of the rainbow. I have no real idea what any of it means but I'm quite impressed that the younger generation understand their colours so well.' She laughed again, delight filling her, and then, because her emotions were so overwrought from being on edge for far too long, she followed Spencer's example and threw her arms around Sean's neck, hugging him close.

'Thank you. Thank you. *Thank you.*'

Sean's arms came easily around her waist and he closed his eyes, allowing her addictive scent to wash over him.

He'd watched Jane throughout her first encounter with Spencer and to be able to offer her such joy and happiness, to unite her with her only living relative, filled Sean's heart with a sense of completeness. As a child, his mother had often told him about the power of giving, of how it made the giver feel happier than the receiver.

Closing his eyes, he tried to commit every second of this spontaneous embrace to memory before Jane pulled back, still grinning up at him, and turned to follow Spencer. There was no doubt in Sean's mind, seeing Spencer talk in his usual animated way, telling Jane all sorts of superfluous things, that it had been the right decision, both for woman and boy. The fact that he himself was drawn to Jane, admiring her intelligence, appreciating her gentleness, accepting her shyness, was the bigger problem.

With Jane now having been introduced to Spencer, it meant that Spencer would classify her as part of his family. It meant that they'd be inviting Jane to their family get-togethers, that he'd be seeing her more and more away from the hospital, in a relaxed, casual setting, and while he was definitely on board with the concept of her enjoying everything his family could offer her, and while he was happy to jump at any excuse to get to know her better, at the back of his mind was the niggling thought that all of this could end in disaster.

The attraction between himself and Jane was very much a fact. At first, he'd thought it was only on his side but after the way she reacted when he'd told her how lovely she was, staring at his mouth and trembling slightly from nervous awareness, Sean was interested to see what would happen if he kissed her.

Even the thought of touching his lips to Jane's made his heart rate increase and yet he questioned himself about the logical implications of such an action. If he were to pursue a romantic relationship with Jane, what would happen if everything went sour? Would he be able to bear seeing her interacting with his family? With his son? Would it be difficult for the two of them to be in the same room together? It would be bad enough at the hospital but at least there they could focus on their patients. However, seeing Jane at his home with Spencer...could he do that? Perhaps it would be better to keep their relationship on a friendly, platonic and professional level to avoid hurting all concerned?

Sean's thoughts continued to spin as he drove home, thankful that Spencer kept up a steady stream of chatter, telling both adults about his day and how Johnny Madalzinski had got into trouble because he'd brought a water squirter to school and squirted the teacher.

'But before he got in trouble we all had a go at lunchtime and when I did it it went the longest and nearly squirted Lanie, and all the boys were jealous because I was the best at it.'

'Does he ever stop for breath?' Jane murmured, and Sean instantly smiled, returning his thoughts to the present.

'Not often.'

As soon as they pulled up in the driveway and Sean garaged the car, Spencer was out of the vehicle like a tornado, picking up his school bag and music bag but dropping bits of paper, a pencil and a lunch wrapper on the ground as he raced into the house. Jane could hear him calling out, 'Grandma? Grandpa? I'm home!'

'He certainly is vibrant and energetic,' Jane remarked as she helped Sean pick up all the things Spencer had dropped.

'He's a healthy, happy, almost-seven-year-old boy.'

Sean gestured to a stool at the kitchen bench. 'Please, have a seat.'

'I can see that.' Jane shook her head in bemusement. 'I just hadn't expected...' She stopped and shrugged as she sat down on the bench stool, watching him turn on his coffee-maker. 'I don't know what I expected.'

'That he'd be like Daina?' Sean asked the question quietly as he took two mugs from the cupboard.

'I don't know. I guess so.' She frowned for a moment. 'It's all so different from how I grew up.'

Sean smiled. 'Not for me. Growing up with two younger sisters in a rowdy but happy home was my normal.'

'It's nice you're able to provide that for Spencer.'

'Some days it's not easy but I have a lot of help and support and that makes all the difference.' He pressed buttons on his impressive coffee-machine and within a minute or two was placing a fresh latte before her. 'I'm guessing your upbringing wasn't exactly normal?'

'No.' Jane stirred the drink and scooped some milk froth up to her lips. She didn't elaborate any further and Sean had to quash his impatience.

Thoughts and questions about Jane had kept him awake for several nights now and maybe if he had some deeper level of understanding of what made Jane Diamond tick, of why she appeared to have such a hold over him, then he'd be able to control the way she made him feel. Sean watched her scoop more milk froth from her drink before licking the spoon. She did this a few times, and one time ended up with froth on her upper lip.

'Wait a sec,' he murmured, and leaned across the bench, brushing her upper lip with his thumb. Jane gasped at the contact, her gaze never leaving his. 'You had a little bit of...' Sean stopped and swallowed, desperately wanting to follow the action with his mouth but knowing that was impossible. Jane was…family now. That was the only way he could allow himself to think of her and yet it was a struggle to do so, especially when she sat there, staring at him with those big, hypnotic green eyes.

He reached out with his other hand and touched her mouth again, his fingers caressing her cheek, his thumb rubbing gently across her lips. Jane sat still, her gaze fixed on his. She was unable to breathe, his touch such a soft caress. His gaze dipped to her mouth. 'I find you quite remarkable, Jane Diamond.'

Before she could say a word he brushed his thumb over her lips again but this time the action was slower, more sensual, more intense. There was no excuse of milk froth, this was just pure desire. It was as though he wanted to touch her, to excite her, to let her see herself through his eyes. But could she trust him?

Jane pushed the thought away, intent on focusing on the here and now as Sean's thumb tenderly traced her lower lip, causing Jane to draw in breath, her entire body flooding with tingles and anticipatory delight.

'I wish you—' She stopped, unable to speak, unable to concentrate, unable to do anything else but feel. Her eyelids fluttered closed. 'You…we…shouldn't,' she whispered, her words barely audible.

'Why shouldn't we?' Sean's words were husky and when she risked opening her eyes to look into his she was stunned to find him looking at her with intense desire. No. That couldn't be right. For so long, for too many years, she'd always believed bad things about herself. She'd been told all her life that she was nothing special, but seeing the way Sean was looking at her…was it possible for her to believe him?

'Jane.' He breathed her name and before she knew what was happening he'd bent his head and brushed a light, feathery kiss across her cheek. 'You clearly have no idea just how much you've infiltrated my thoughts.' He continued to kiss her face, edging his way towards her ear, and Jane couldn't help the tears that instantly sprang to her eyes and began to slide down her cheek.

Sean kept kissing her face, working his way up to her forehead, before he looked at her. 'Jane, you're a beautiful woman.'

She shook her head but he stilled the movement, wiping away her tears. 'Say the words,' he instructed softly. 'Say, "I am a beautiful woman."'

'I can't.'

'But it's true and I think you need to start believing it. I wouldn't say it otherwise.'

'Ha!' She laughed without humour.

'If you don't believe I'm telling the truth, you must think I'm lying.'

Jane's answer to this statement was to shrug her shoulders.

'So you think I'm lying.'

'Men have lied before in order to seduce a woman.'

'You think I'm trying to seduce you?' His eyebrows hit his hairline.

'Aren't you?'

'With my son and parents not too far away?' he said, and she had to concede his point.

'You still didn't answer the question,' she said softly.

He chuckled softly and she edged back from his tender touch, trying to block out his sweet words. She knew there was no way he could really mean them and she'd learnt long ago not to build up false hopes.

'You're a smart woman, Jane, so how come, when it comes to affairs of the heart, you just clam up?'

'Sean…' There was the hint of protest in her tone, indicating she wasn't sure about the course this conversation was taking, but when he smiled at her she found her mind turning to mush and she completely forgot what she'd been about to say. How was it possible he could make her do that? She'd always been able to maintain a certain level of control over her emotions as far as men were concerned. Even with Eamon she'd been the one to call the shots in the relationship, which had been one of the reasons he'd cited when he'd broken their engagement.

'Hmm?' He exhaled slowly, his gaze flicking from her eyes to her lips, the action causing Jane to feel all tingly inside, her heart rate increasing. 'You are stunning.'

'Don't look at me like that,' she protested weakly.

'Like what? Like a man who's very interested in you?'

He wanted to kiss her. He wanted to kiss her and the desire was increasing with each passing second, especially when she continued to stare at him with those gorgeous eyes of hers.

'Don't be interested in me.'

'Why not?'

'Because I...' She stopped and swallowed, her gaze lingering on his mouth for just a fraction of a second longer than it should have. It was enough to let him know that even though she was saying no, deep inside her heart she was saying yes. It was enough to give him hope and he hadn't felt hope about a relationship for a very long time now. He also knew it was important for Jane to steer them through these tentative waters at her own pace. Rushing would only result in her rejecting him and he'd been rejected enough to last a lifetime.

'Jane—' he tried hard not to stare at her luscious lips as he spoke '—I want you to know that I take my commitments very seriously and—'

'Stop.' Jane placed a finger across his lips. 'Don't say

anything, Sean. Don't make any promises.' She quickly removed her finger, the intimate contact doing nothing to quell the simmering fires of desire burning through her entire body. She really did want to believe what Sean was saying, wanted to accept him at his word, but how could she when she'd trusted in the past and been hurt? If Sean knew the truth of her secret, if he comprehended that she really wasn't beautiful at all, if he saw her terrible sca—

'Jane?' he queried.

'I…I'm just not sure I can deal with reje—'

'Through here!' came Spencer's loud, excited voice, heading in their direction. 'You'll never believe it, Grandma. *Another* aunty!'

Within a split second of hearing Spencer's voice Jane had pushed Sean away, needing to put as much distance between them as possible, and slipped off the stool. She tried to quieten her frantic thoughts. How could she have possibly allowed Sean to get so close?

She tugged at her top, making sure it was in place, instantly wishing she hadn't come dressed so casually. She combed her fringe with her fingers and pulled the long plaits, which Sean had pushed back, to the front. It was her armour and right now. With the impending prospect of meeting Sean's parents, she needed it more than ever. She had no idea what sort of reception they might give the sister of the woman who, from the few things Sean had said, had caused their son a fair amount of emotional stress. Would they tar her with the same brush?

'Look. See?' Spencer ran towards where his father and Jane were standing. 'Another aunty! From my mummy's side.'

The little boy sounded so excited, not at all perturbed that his words might cause painful memories to resurface.

He ran right up to her, glancing back now and then to ensure his grandparents were following.

Jane, now satisfied that her 'armour' was on, stood her ground, ready to be introduced to the two people walking towards her. Sean's mother had short dark hair with red and gold streaks through it, and his father was the spitting image of his son, only thirty years older. If he was any indication of how Sean would age, Jane had to admit that there were some excellent genes in the Booke family gene pool.

'You were right, Spencer,' Sean's mother remarked as she walked over to where Jane stood. Sean just leaned against the bench top and watched as his mother smiled brightly. 'Hello. Sean told us you'd be stopping by.'

Jane squared her shoulders and lifted her chin, pasting a professional smile on her face. 'I hope it's not an inconvenience?'

'Oh, tush,' his mother said, and brushed Jane's words away. Still, Jane wasn't exactly sure what to do or say next so she held out her hand. 'I'm Jane. It's a pleasure to meet you, Mrs Booke.'

'Good heavens. Call me Louise. We're hardly that formal, isn't that right, Barney?' she said, glancing at her husband. Barney shook hands with Jane after Louise, the two of them staring at her for what seemed like an eternity but which in reality was only a few seconds.

'I do hope you're able to stay for dinner, Jane.' Louise glanced at Sean, who shrugged. 'You haven't even asked Jane to dinner yet? Where are your manners?' Louise swatted playfully at her son.

'Yeah, Dad,' Spencer took the opportunity to chime in, a cheeky grin on his face. 'Manners!'

Jane couldn't help the bubble of laughter that overflowed and she quickly clapped a hand over her mouth.

A split second later both Sean and his parents laughed as well and Spencer just stood there, grinning, pleased the adults were laughing but not at all sure why.

'So…dinner?' Louise persisted, leaning in closer. 'Let me give you a little tip. I won't take no for an answer.'

'Then I guess…' Jane said, quickly glancing at Sean to make sure it was all right with him. When he gave her a small nod she realised he was more than happy to have her stay. 'I'd better not say no.'

'Excellent. OK, Spencer, we need to set the table.'

Spencer raced off, calling loudly, 'But I can do it by myself. I'm nearly seven, you know.'

'I'll help him,' Barney said, and Jane had to admit that for a man in his seventies he was quite spry.

'Now, why don't I show you the house,' Louise stated, and then, before Jane knew what was happening, Louise had linked her arm through hers and was leading her towards the staircase. 'We live in the upstairs part of the house and Spencer and Sean live downstairs. That way, if Sean gets called to the hospital in the middle of the night, he doesn't need to disturb Spencer,' Louise said, and Jane turned and glanced back at Sean, her eyes wide with uncertainty. Sean's answer to her unspoken question was to give her a friendly wave.

At first she felt as though Sean was feeding her to the lions but after a few minutes in Louise's company she realised the woman was gentle and genuine. She talked about how Sean had insisted they all live together. 'It works well for all of us because Barney and I aren't getting any younger and it pays to be living close to a doctor should we need him.' She laughed and it was only then that Jane realised she was joking.

'Come and help me with dinner.'

'Are we ready to eat yet, Grandma?' Spencer asked,

and Jane was amazed not only at his manners but also his easygoing relationship with his grandmother. Jane couldn't even remember meeting her grandparents and never had she interacted with her own parents in such a relaxed and friendly manner. Children had been treated very differently in her family.

She watched as Spencer helped his grandmother, the two of them laughing easily together. When Sean and his father joined them, the atmosphere only became more relaxed. She sat quietly throughout the meal, only really speaking when spoken to but watching with pleased astonishment the genuine familial love demonstrated by the Booke family.

'So, Jane,' Louise asked, as she and Spencer dished up a dessert of fresh fruit and home-made ice cream, 'what is it that's brought you back to Adelaide?'

Jane instantly looked at Sean, wondering if she should confess she'd moved here because of Spencer, that she was all alone in the world and he was all she had left in the way of family. If she said that, however, she knew Louise and Barney would feel sorry for her and, besides, she didn't want Spencer to feel obligated to get to know her.

'Uh...'

'She was head-hunted by the hospital,' Sean put in, holding Jane's gaze firmly. 'You see, Mum, Jane's a brilliant paediatrician who has been involved in extensive research with juvenile eating disorders.'

'Really? Head-hunted?'

'That's impressive,' Barney added.

Jane wasn't used to so much positive attention and quietly thanked them before eating more of her dessert so she didn't have to answer any more questions.

'So, are you married or have a steady boyfriend?' Louise asked.

'Mum!' Sean's reaction was one of instant mortification.

'What?' Louise spread her arms wide, feigning innocence. 'Jane's part of our family now and I have a right to know a bit more about the members of my family. It's not an uncommon question, Sean.'

Jane's spoon clattered to the table and she swallowed over the instant lump in her throat. 'Part of...' She stopped, unable to believe how warmed her heart became at those words.

'Our family,' Louise finished, with a wide smile. 'You're Spencer's aunt. That makes you family and we Bookes take our family ties very seriously. We like being involved in each other's lives and helping out and caring and loving. It's what families do.'

Jane could feel Sean watching her closely. He knew the truth. He knew why she'd really returned to Adelaide. To hear his mother welcome her so openly, so freely, especially after only having met her less than an hour ago, made Jane feel a warmth flood through her, a caring, loving warmth such as she'd never felt before.

'You might be smothering her a bit, Mum,' Sean murmured under his breath, but Jane set her shoulders straight and looked at Louise.

'No. This isn't smothering. Not in the slightest. I guess I'm just a little surprised that you're so interested in me.'

'Why wouldn't we be?' Louise asked.

'Because...' Jane paused and glanced once at Sean before drawing in a deep breath, his small nod of encouragement giving her strength to continue. 'Because I've been on my own ever since Daina died. I came from a very dysfunctional family and have no idea what a normal family is supposed to be like. I have no husband, no fiancé and no boyfriend. In fact, I have no other family except Spencer.' Her gaze fell on the small boy and she smiled warmly. 'He's my only relative.'

'Only? Oh, my dear,' Louise said softly, her tone filled with maternal concern. She immediately came around to where Jane was seated and tugged her to her feet. 'Jane, Jane, you poor thing.' Louise held both of Jane's hands in hers. 'You may have been alone and without family when you walked in this door tonight, but right here, right now, that changes.'

'Yes,' Barney agreed, coming to stand by his wife.

'*We* are your family.' And with that Louise put her arms around Jane and hugged her close. Barney put his arm around both women and in another instant Spencer was wrapping his little arms around her waist.

Jane, a little startled from such open displays of affection but also absorbing every moment of it, looked across to where Sean sat, a big, wide grin on his face.

He winked at her. 'Welcome to the family, Jane.'

CHAPTER EIGHT

JANE INSISTED ON taking a taxi home after dinner, especially as Sean still needed to settle Spencer down after his exciting evening, gaining a new family member.

'Mum and Dad can put him to bed and I can drive you back to the res wing,' he offered, but she put her phone away after dialling the number for the cab company.

'It's fine. You've already given me so much today and I don't want to overstay my welcome.'

'Impossible.'

'Still, I can't thank you enough, Sean.' Her face was radiant as she looked at him and he clenched his jaw and shoved his hands into his trouser pockets to stop himself from hauling her close into a warm and comforting hug.

'It's good to see you smiling, Jane.'

'Why wouldn't I smile?' She spread her arms wide. 'This is close to being the best day of my life.'

'Really?'

'Well, I don't want to say it's the very best day because who knows, there may be better ones yet to come, but for now this day is definitely first.'

'I'm glad.' And he was. What she must have been through over the years and yet she'd managed to conquer so many negative emotions, and all on her own?

Jane watched him closely, noticing a slight frown mar his brow. 'You don't...you know...mind, do you?'

'Mind?'

'Sharing your family with me,' she answered.

Sean's smile was honest and forthright. 'It's a pleasure, Jane.' It also meant that because his family had welcomed her, effectively adopting her as one of their own, he would need to work better at controlling his wayward senses whenever she was around. Even now, the desire to hug her, especially when she was just standing there, looking up at him as though he'd given her the moon, was still difficult for him to resist. From what he'd seen and from what she'd shared, Jane clearly needed stability in her life and any sort of romantic attachment he may feel towards her was null and void.

Colleagues. Friends. Family. That would be his relationship with her from now on.

'Did you want to say goodnight to Spencer?' Sean offered as he took a step back from her, and Jane immediately nodded. The little boy begged her to read him a story while she waited for her taxi to come and this she did, unable to believe the joy she felt at being able to do such a simple, ordinary task.

When she'd finished, he put up his hands to her, indicating he wanted her to pick him up. She put her arms around him and he gave her the biggest, squeeziest hug she'd ever had in her life.

'I'm so excited to go shopping for my birthday present,' he said, and Jane almost toppled backwards from the way he was leaning in to her.

'So am I,' she returned, the warmth inside her increasing when Spencer kissed her cheek. When the taxi pulled up, Sean stepped forward and lifted his son up and into his arms, Spencer more than comfortable resting his head

against his father's broad shoulder. Jane wanted to pull out
her cellphone, to take a photo of man and boy, especially
given their similar colouring. Instead, she smiled at them
both, before turning and walking out into the waning late
February sunshine to where the taxi was waiting.

'See you tomorrow morning for ward round,' Sean
called, and she turned to wave.

'See you next weekend at the beach,' Spencer called,
giggling as he tried to imitate his father's deep tones.

'The beach?' Jane was confused.

'I'll talk to you about it tomorrow at ward round,' Sean
told her, and she nodded, excitement filling her at the prospect of seeing more of the Booke family.

Jane couldn't help but giggle a little herself as she waved
one last time and climbed into the back seat of the taxi.
She gave the driver the address then buckled her seat belt
and closed her eyes, allowing the wonderful warmth of
memories to wash over her. For so long she'd imagined
what it might be like to be included in such a close-knit
family unit, fanciful dreams she'd had throughout childhood, and tonight, thanks to Sean's graciousness, she had
felt the full power of familial love.

Not only that but somehow she'd found herself drawing
closer and closer to the man himself, still unable to believe
he'd almost kissed her. Was it possible she'd finally found
a man who really could see beneath the shields she'd taken
great pains to erect? The fact that he knew some things
about her past had helped. It had provided them with a
bond, right from the start, and even though they'd both
been a little sceptical of the other, they'd somehow managed to find common ground.

The butterflies in her stomach took flight as she recalled the way Sean had stared longingly into her eyes,
of the way his gaze had dipped to her lips as though he'd

wanted nothing more than to cover them with his own. And perhaps he would have, if they hadn't been interrupted.

Would she have pushed him away? Would she have welcomed his embrace? Even just thinking about it now was causing her to tremble with anticipation. What if he had kissed her and it hadn't been any good? What if the sensual tension she felt when she stared into his beautiful blue eyes only affected her and not him?

She stopped that thought before it could take root. Negative thoughts only bred negative emotions. That was something she'd learned a long time ago and she wouldn't allow them to infiltrate the happiness she'd found tonight. Sean was a handsome and wonderful man and perhaps, at some point in the future, there might be the possibility that he would give in to the repressed desire she'd witnessed in his eyes and capture her lips with his own. When he did, she wanted to be ready, wanted to let him know that he was exciting sensations and feelings within her she'd never really felt before. To let him know that how he made her feel was unique.

When she arrived at the residential wing, she paid the taxi driver and entered the building with a definite spring in her step and a wide smile on her lips. Happiness was an emotion she'd searched hard to find and yet tonight she felt as though she'd been given a huge dose and it was a sensation she was determined to hang onto.

For the next week Jane felt as though she was walking on air. Sean had spoken to her about his family's plans to head to the beach the following Saturday.

'As part of the family, you're expected to attend.'

'Oh. Uh…OK.'

He'd laughed at the uncertainty reflected on her face. 'Relax, Jane. You'll be fine. Trust me.' Then he'd winked at her and headed to his next meeting. In fact, throughout the week Sean had definitely appeared to be treating her in a more brotherly way. He made no effort to touch her again and she started to wonder whether he still found her attractive?

He kept to his word about Spencer and so far she'd seen her nephew three times during the week, dining again with them on Wednesday night. This time, Spencer had insisted she read him three stories and when Sean told his son that Jane had a lovely singing voice, Spencer had insisted she sing to him.

'You have to be lying down, teeth brushed and ready for bed,' his father had ordered, and Spencer had quickly gone through his night-time routine, eager to have Jane sing to him. Spencer had asked her to lie down on the bed next to him and with an encouraging nod from Sean, who'd been watching from the doorway, she'd kicked off her shoes and rested her head on the pillow beside Spencer. Then the boy had surprised her even further by wrapping his little arms about her neck and snuggling in close.

'OK, Aunty Jane. I'm ready for you to sing now,' he'd told her, but it had taken Jane a moment or two to clear the sudden lump of emotion from her throat before filling the room with her beautiful song. Spencer's easy acceptance, his easy love was going a long way to opening up a heart she'd kept closed for a very long time. And it wasn't only Spencer who was working his magic. Thoughts of Sean seemed to be her constant companions and she'd started to realise it was pointless to deny them. She *wanted* to think about him, she *liked* thinking about him, but most of all she desperately hoped that he was thinking about her in return.

She sang three songs to Spencer and at the end of the third one realised the boy was asleep, his breathing nice and steady.

'Uh...Sean?' she whispered.

'Yeah?'

'I'm stuck.' Although he was sleeping soundly, Spencer's arms were still firmly around her neck. 'How do I get up without waking him?'

Sean's soft chuckle washed over her before he came to her rescue, shifting his son out of the way before helping Jane to her feet. The two of them were standing very close, her hands on his upper arms, her fingers tingling from the feel of his firm biceps beneath his shirt. He placed his hands at her waist to steady her and as she stood there, her toes curling into the soft rug, her knees threatening to fail her, Jane stared into his face with a feeling of homecoming.

The two of them, standing here, close together, beside Spencer's bed, the little boy sleeping—it all felt as though this was where she was meant to be. It felt right. Although his face was half-lit by the shadows created by Spencer's nightlight, Jane had the sense that Sean felt it, too. They stayed there, neither of them moving, for half a minute, the character clock on the wall ticking in time with her heartbeat.

There was no panic, no questions, no need to search for ulterior motives. The moment was...perfect. Even when Sean took her hand in his, letting her slip on her shoes before he led her from the room, Jane felt no sense of apprehension or fear. Yet when the bright artificial light from the kitchen made them both squint, Sean dropped her hand before heading around to fill the kettle, offering her a cup of tea.

'No, thanks,' she said, realising he was once more trying to inject some distance between them. 'I'd better call for a taxi.'

'OK.' He didn't try to talk her out of it, didn't offer to drive her home, and when he walked her to the taxi and shut the door, she saw him shove both of his hands through his hair before sighing heavily and heading back inside. What the action had meant she wasn't sure but his happy, brotherly attention towards her had continued, leaving Jane feeling quite confused.

On Friday, just after she finished morning clinic and was on her way to the ward conference room for a progress meeting about Tessa, her cellphone buzzed in her pocket. Jane was astonished to find it was Louise.

'Hello, Jane.' Louise's bright tones came down the line. 'Just wanted to let you know about the plans for tomorrow at the beach. Barney has a great gazebo he likes to put up on the sand so we'll have some shade and the girls have some lovely recliner chairs, which means you don't get sand all over you when you lie down. Now, with regard to food,' Louise continued, before Jane could get a word in edge ways, 'we figured cold cuts of meat and salad should be the order of the day. Sean's bringing the drinks and I was hoping you'd be able to provide some sort of dessert, perhaps a fruit bun or some fresh fruit, nothing that's going to melt or go stale too quickly in such extreme heat. What do you think?'

Jane gaped a few times as Louise talked and then quickly agreed. 'I'd be delighted to provide something for dessert. Thank you for the suggestions.'

'All right, dear, no doubt you're as busy as anything so I'll let you go. See you tomorrow—patients willing.'

Jane couldn't help but giggle with happiness as she said goodbye, ending the call and slipping her phone back into her pocket.

'That sounded like a nice phone call,' Sean's deep voice said from just behind her. Jane turned and looked over her shoulder, waiting for him to catch up.

'That was your mother.'

'Oh?'

'Yes. Organising tomorrow's *family* event.' Jane grinned as she enunciated the words clearly, the smile on her face growing brighter. 'She wants me to provide something for dessert.' The pride in her words was clearly evident.

'Excellent. Make it something chocolate.'

'Chocolate?' Jane frowned. 'But won't that melt?'

'Not if you put it in the drinks cooler I'm bringing. I'll have lots of ice in there.'

'Oh. Well, Louise suggested a fruit bun or some fresh fruit and I don't want to take the wrong thing.' Her frown increased. 'This is the very first time I've ever been asked to contribute something to a *family* event and I don't want to mess it up. It means I'm included, not just a guest joining in for the day.' She paused. 'Perhaps I should bring fruit bun and fresh fruit and chocolate.'

Sean chuckled. 'You're over-thinking this, Jane.'

'Well, wouldn't you?' she asked as they entered the ward.

'It won't matter what you bring, everyone will be appreciative. Trust me. Both of my sisters are health freaks and their children and husbands will thank you for bringing along a bit of chocolate.'

Jane shook her head slowly. 'You think you're helping me, Sean, but you're just making me even more confused. The last thing I want to do, the very first time I meet your sisters, is to get them off side.'

'Impossible. They'll love you.' He winked at her and the resident butterflies in her stomach took flight. Stupid butterflies.

'Good. Then *you* bring the chocolate,' she remarked, and again his warm chuckle filled her with pleasure. She really had to figure out how to get better control over her senses, especially when it appeared Sean really did think of her more as a sister than anything else. She pushed the thought away and focused on the meeting, eager to receive progress reports about Tessa's situation.

After the meeting Jane went to have a chat with Tessa, pleased when the little girl smiled warmly at the sight of her. Sean watched as Tessa leaned in close to Jane, talking softly but earnestly, opening up more, confiding, confessing.

There was certainly something engaging about Jane, about the way she gave you one hundred per cent of her attention when she was talking to you or listening to you. Even his mother had remarked about it.

'She's so…interested in everything,' Louise had said yesterday morning at breakfast. 'You did the right thing, Sean, inviting her to be a part of Spencer's life. You didn't have to.'

'It was the right thing to do.' Even though it meant he'd been unable to get her out of his mind ever since. Last night, for instance, he'd found himself waking up at three o'clock in the morning from a dream where he'd been holding her close, in one of the outpatient clinic rooms, kissing her perfect mouth, unable to resist her any longer.

He told himself he was happy she'd been accepted by his family; both his sisters were very eager to meet her. Getting his own urges under control was paramount, especially when Jane kept smiling brightly at him simply because she'd been asked to bring some food to a family picnic.

Yet when he knocked on her door on Saturday morning to pick her up and take her to the beach, it was a very different, less composed Jane who opened the door.

'I've bought an Esky and packed the food into it, as you suggested,' she dithered, not bothering to invite him in but leaving the door wide open, indicating he should feel free to cross the threshold. The large red insulated cold box was by the door, ready to just pick up when they left.

'I bought a sun hat,' she continued, pointing to the large, almost sombrero-like hat on the bed. 'And some strong sunscreen, but now I can't find where I put it.' She opened a drawer and searched inside, before closing it and opening the next one. 'You would think, in such a confined space as this, I wouldn't lose anything!' Exasperation laced through her tone as she once more did the rounds of the room, stopping for a brief moment to look at and around him. 'Where's Spencer?'

'He's going with my parents. I wanted to stop by the ward and check on some patients.'

'Oh. Of course.' Jane tried to disguise her disappointment at not being able to spend even a few more minutes with Spencer. She opened her wardrobe doors and looked in there for the sunscreen, although why she would have put it in there, she had no clue.

Sean scanned the room as well, trying not to be intrigued by what she was wearing. Most people, on such a stinking hot day as this, would wear fewer clothes. Shorts and T-shirt or, for a woman, a light cotton sundress with flip-flops, but not Jane. She was dressed in a pair of light-coloured three-quarter-length trousers, a pastel top and a thin cotton long-sleeve shirt over the top. Her hair...even as he watched her flit around the room...mesmerised him. Her fringe was, as always, combed over her forehead, coming down to meet her eyebrows, but the long, luscious locks were contained in some sort of messy braided low bun, little wisps of hair falling out here and there, framing her face and making her look...angelic.

His gut tightened with the urge to stop her, to pull her close, to calm her nerves—which were clearly on display with all her dithering—and enfold her in his arms. He wanted to reassure her that she was safe, that he would never let anyone hurt her, and he wanted to follow the lead of the constant dreams he'd been having of her where he would tenderly capture her lips with his.

'Jane, I have some sunscreen,' he told her softly, as she checked beneath the bed.

'But this is special stuff. I burn so easily,' she told him, and when she straightened, meeting his gaze, he realised the extent of her nervousness. She looked terrified and he realised that although she was excited to be a part of a family, it was also very new and unsettling to her. He instantly stepped forward and gathered her hands in his. It was the first time he'd touched her in so long that he felt like he'd been struck by lightning. What this woman did to him, how she affected him, was becoming even more powerful than before.

Sean quickly settled his thoughts before speaking. 'Jane, it's no drama.'

His calm, easy words, the warmth from his touch, the way he gave her that handsome half-smile instantly melted her nerves. How was it possible that in the blink of an eye Sean Booke was able to quell her fears and to make her feel so incredibly safe?

'It isn't?'

'No. We can buy some more along the way. You're supposed to be relaxing today, on your day off from the hospital, not stressing about sunscreen.'

'But—'

'Shh,' he interrupted and placed a finger across her lips. He knew it was a stupid move the moment his skin made contact with hers because even touching her in such a way made it nigh on impossible for him to continue to keep his distance, for him to try and view her as some sort of distant relative.

The sensations he'd been doing his best to quash for the past week came bursting forth. 'I've tried so hard to keep my distance, to see you as just another family member but...' he shook his head slowly '...it isn't working. I can't stop thinking about you.'

'Oh.' She sighed, trembling slightly at his words, her body tingling with delight. She licked her lips then swallowed.

'Why do you think I haven't touched you? And made sure I wasn't alone with you in a room? I just couldn't control my reaction to you.'

Was that why? Was he telling the truth? Jane swallowed, unable to speak for a moment while her mind processed this information.

'But, Sean...' She stopped, staring into his eyes and taking a deep breath as she realised it was time to perhaps ask some tricky questions, to take a few bricks out of the protective wall she'd carefully constructed around herself. 'Sean, are we...I mean, do we...you know, *feel* the way we do simply because of that past connection?'

'Or are we *attracted*—' Sean spoke the word clearly and pointedly, indicating he knew what she'd been trying to say and that he wasn't afraid to name what they both clearly felt '—to each other because we're so much alike?'

Was that the reason? She'd never thought of it like that before but, then, she'd been attempting to school her thoughts where Sean was concerned. She had such an innate fear that if she gave herself permission to really explore this attraction and then somehow messed things up, he would cut her off from ever seeing Spencer again.

'You're trembling,' he pointed out, rubbing his thumbs over her hands.

'I'm nervous about meeting your sisters, of making a good impression, of having this day go well,' she babbled, looking away from his hypnotic gaze in case he saw the truth, that she was frightened of the way he made her feel.

'You don't need to worry about my sisters. They're pre-disposed to like you.'

'Why? How do you know that?' Jane tried to gently tug her hands free from the touch that was setting her senses on fire.

Sean chuckled softly, the sound warming her through and through. 'Because I know my sisters and I know you.'

'No, you don't.' This time she did pull away and turned her back to him. Sean immediately put his hands on her shoulders, rubbing her arms as he spoke in that soothing voice of his.

'I know you better than most,' he countered. 'And I like what I see, Jane. I like you…a lot.'

CHAPTER NINE

BY THE TIME they arrived at the beach, Jane was a mass of nerves. Not only was she about to meet Sean's sisters and their families but he'd just confessed to her that he liked her—a lot. He was attracted to her and she had no present concept of what that meant, what he now expected of her, and whether or not she'd be able to fulfil it.

She decided to focus on the immediate problem of making a good impression on Sean's sisters, Rosie and Kathleen, but, as Sean had predicted, they were already enamoured with her from the start, both of them coming forward to hug her and welcome her to their family. Spencer's greeting was to launch himself at her like a cannon ball, give her a firm hug before wriggling from her arms to run off and play with his cousins, who were tossing a ball to each other.

Barney and Louise also welcomed her with hugs and after a few hours of sitting around, chatting and eating and laughing, Jane couldn't help but smile brightly.

'I could get used to this,' she remarked to Sean, as he sat down beside her on the towel she'd spread on the golden sand. Louise and Barney were nearby, lounging on the chairs, chatting with one of their daughters, so Jane spoke softly.

'What? Sweat all day because the sun's too hot? Or

having to reapply sunscreen every few hours? Or craving salty foods due to the sea salt in the air? Or perhaps it's the constant swatting of flies you could get used to?'

Jane laughed. 'All of the above, as well as being surrounded by people who are happy to be with me.'

These words told him far more about her upbringing, about the loneliness she'd faced as an adult, than if she'd told him directly. He wanted to reassure her, to let her know that her days of being alone were over. 'We are, Jane. We all are and it's genuine.'

She turned to look at him and even though she was wearing prescription sunglasses, she knew the lenses weren't dark enough that he couldn't see her eyes. 'I really want to believe that, Sean. It's been very difficult for me to take that leap of faith and to trust but today I really do feel accepted.'

'I'm glad.' He stared at her for a moment before forcing himself to look away, her smiling mouth far too tempting, and here was most definitely not the place for their first real kiss. He knew it was inevitable, that soon he would kiss Jane, and he wanted it to be perfect.

Spencer came running up, interrupting the moment, demanding his father come into the sea and 'toss him around'.

'Toss him around?' Jane looked at Sean as he stood, trying not to stare as he pulled off his T-shirt, revealing a very broad, very brawny, very beautiful chest. Her fingers instantly began to tingle, wanting to touch it, to feel the light smattering of hair on his chest. She unconsciously licked her lips and breathed out slowly as she carefully raised her gaze back to meet his. It was only then she realised he'd been more than aware of her visual caress and that he'd enjoyed every second of it. The gorgeous little half-smile that set her heart racing once more was firmly in place. He raised one eyebrow, indicating he was very interested in her interest in him.

'Why don't you come and join us?' Sean asked, scooping his son into his arms, mainly to stop Spencer from excitedly jumping up and down and spraying sand all over Jane, and also because to have her look at him in such a way had been extremely alluring.

'Yeah. Aunty Jane, Aunty Jane, Aunty Jane. Come in the sea with us!' Spencer clapped his hands and giggled with anticipatory delight.

'Uh...' Jane quickly shook her head and looked away from the perfect picture of man and boy, two sets of perfect blue eyes enticing her to join them. 'I don't like the water.' And as she said the words she unconsciously adjusted her glasses and tugged at the hem of her cotton shirt, before ensuring the sleeves of the shirt were still secured at her wrists.

'Aw. Why not?' Spencer was clearly disappointed and it was the last thing Jane wanted. She thought fast and knew she had to do something to appease him but she was not going into that water. Wearing a swimsuit would only expose the rest of the people on the beach to her body. She didn't want to be stared at or thought a freak. She'd suffered through enough of that for years and now that she was her own, strong, independent self, she was the one deciding what she would and wouldn't do, and she would not go into that water and swim.

'Why don't you come and stand in the shallows?' Sean suggested, and when she looked at him, she realised he'd been watching her entire internal struggle. 'Just roll your trousers up a bit and paddle in the shallows.'

'Yeah!' Spencer clapped his hands in agreement.

Jane nodded, realising Sean had provided the perfect solution. She'd get to join in, to find out what 'tossing Spencer around' consisted of. She quickly located her enormous hat and placed it on her head, before following Sean's suggestion and rolling up her trousers to just above her knees. She stood and brushed sand from her clothes.

'Ready?' Sean asked, before putting Spencer down and holding out his hand to her.

'Ready,' she stated, and took his hand, drawing in a cleansing breath. Sean was asking her to join in but he wasn't forcing her to do anything she wasn't comfortable with. Did he have any idea just how much that endeared him to her? It let her know that he was willing to accept her for what she could give. Wasn't that what she'd been searching for? Acceptance?

Smiling brightly at him, she walked quickly across the hot sand to where the water was lapping. Spencer ran full pelt into the water, splashing with the waves and laughing brightly. Sean raised Jane's hand to his lips and pressed a kiss to it before letting her go and following his son, scooping the giggling boy up and wading with him to the deeper water.

Jane clasped her hands together, her thumb consciously rubbing the spot where he'd kissed her as she allowed the delight to wash over her. Did he realise that such a small, respectful and charming gesture as that would only make her like him even more?

When the water was up to Sean's waist, and he had made sure that the coast was clear, Jane watched as Sean faced Spencer away from him and then, on the count of three, tossed his son into the air, the little boy whooping with delight before he splashed into the water not too far away.

Sean turned to face Jane and spread his hands wide as if to say, 'Ta-dah!' She laughed and clapped and gave him a thumbs-up as Spencer swam back to his father, ready for a repeat performance.

'Hey! Look!' she heard some of Spencer's cousins say. 'Uncle Sean's tossing Spencer. Come on.'

'It's my turn after Spencer,' one of them called.

'I'm after you,' the other yelled, as they made their way out to Sean. Jane laughed, more than happy to watch. After a while Louise came and stood beside her, the two of them both cheering and clapping as Sean patiently 'tossed' his son, his nephews and niece into the water.

Jane couldn't believe how relaxed she felt around this close-knit family, how accepted she felt, and she knew it was all because of Sean. Even later in the afternoon, as he drove her home, the conversation was easy and relaxed.

'Does Spencer often go to his cousins' house for sleepovers?' she asked as Sean concentrated on the heavier-than-usual traffic.

'At least once a month, or I have a few of them at my house on the weekend, depending on sporting schedules. It's good for Spencer to mix with his cousins, especially being an only child.' He frowned a little as he slowed the car. 'Fair dinkum, I think everyone left the beach to head home at the same time,' he murmured a moment later.

'Would you like more children?' she asked with soft intrigue, pleased he'd provided her with the perfect opening to ask the question.

'I like being a father,' Sean commented as he changed lanes. 'But raising a child, especially when my parenting career began with having the sole care of a sick, premature baby, wasn't at all easy. That's when my parents and I came up with the living arrangements we now have. We both sold our places and converted the house, ensuring they had their own separate living quarters and I had mine but that Spencer's needs could easily be met.'

'So what happens when he wakes up in the morning and you're at the hospital?'

'There's a message board in my parents' kitchen. You might have seen it. I usually leave a message on there, letting them know I'm not home. My dad's an early riser so if Spencer wakes up and I'm not in my bedroom, he just goes upstairs and his grandparents look after him.' Sean shrugged. 'It's the best solution we could come up with.'

'I think it's a wonderful solution and I'm sure your parents love spending so much time with their grandson.'

Spencer grinned. 'They do, and vice versa. We all just wanted to make Spencer's life as easy and uncomplicated as possible.'

Jane paused before asking the question that had been bothering her for some time. 'Does he ever ask about Daina?'

'Not really. He was three when Daina passed away but she left home soon after he was born, and he doesn't remember her.' They were silent for a moment, Sean inching the car forward in traffic then stopping due to the gridlock. 'Jane…when was the last time you saw her?'

Jane looked out the window for a moment, not really seeing the sea of cars before them but instead calling up her old memories. The topic of her sister was hardly her favourite subject but if she wanted things to progress with Sean, perhaps it was best they dealt with questions when they arose naturally.

'I believe it was about four months after she'd come to see me about wanting me to terminate her pregnancy.' She stared down at her hands, surprised to find them quite relaxed. Usually when she spoke about Daina her hands would be clenched tightly together, but not this time. Was it because she knew that, whatever she said, Sean would accept her words as truth?

'She turned up on my doorstep in Melbourne, no baby in tow. Figure back to perfection. She said she was flying overseas the next day and just needed to stay for the night. She was more than happy to show me one or two pictures of Spencer, to rub in the fact that she still had everything. She was married and she had a baby and I was still her weird freak of a sister, who would always be alone. That was the first I knew of Spencer's name and his birth date. She said he was still in hospital and she didn't have time to sit and wait around. That she'd met a modelling producer and he wanted to do a professional photographic session with her in Bali. She left early the next morning and I heard nothing else until two days before her funeral, and even then it was quite by accident.'

Jane shook her head. 'I found out my sister had died because I bumped into a friend of hers. She was distraught, calling me unfeeling and ungracious, especially after everything Daina had done for me. I had no idea what she was going on about until she told me Daina had been killed in a car accident.'

'Jane.' Sean looked to her, a worried frown on his brow. 'I'm sorry. I would have told you but I had no idea where you lived or how to contact you or anything.'

Jane shook her head. 'It's over. Her death made it over. As horrible as it is to say, with Daina gone I knew she wouldn't be able to hurt me any more.'

Sean reached over and cupped her face with his hand, the warmth of his touch, the caress of his fingers making her heart soar with possibilities. 'It is over,' he agreed. 'And we are free to move forward with our lives.' His smile was encouraging, promising and with a small hint of excitement in his eyes. He dropped his hand and looked back at the traffic before them. The light had turned green but no one had moved, the intersection blocked with other cars. 'Something's wrong.'

Jane noticed the change in his tone of voice and when she looked out at the gridlocked traffic, she frowned. 'Roadworks?'

'Or an accident.' Sean reached for his cellphone and called through to the Adelaide General Hospital. He spoke for a moment to a colleague in the emergency department. 'The ambulances can't get through,' he told Jane as he waited another moment for further information. 'We're close,' he told the person on the other end of the phone. 'Right. OK. No problem.' He made sure they had his cellphone number before he disconnected the call and drove his car up onto the wide grassed median strip in the middle of the road.

'We'll have to help out,' he told Jane as he unbuckled his seat belt.

Jane swallowed as she felt all the colour drain from her face, dizziness swamping her. 'A car accident?' Her words were barely a whisper.

Sean shifted in his seat to look at her. 'Jane, I know attending a car accident must be difficult for you because you lost your parents in a car accident, didn't you? Or was that another one of Daina's fabrications?'

'No. That was true but…' Jane swallowed her words. How could she explain to Sean what she'd endured? All those surgeries, being in and out of hospital…the pain. She closed her eyes and tried to focus her wayward thoughts. Facts. Focus on the facts. There was a car accident. People were hurt, they were in pain, just as she'd been. Jane knew if it hadn't been for the paramedics who had attended her at the accident site, using their knowledge and expertise to save her, she would not have survived. Wasn't it only right that she now did the same for others who needed her, used her own knowledge and expertise to make a radical difference to someone's life?

She opened her eyes, looking directly at Sean. 'Those people need our help,' she stated, more to get the words through her own foggy mind than to point out the obvious.

'Yes.'

Jane clutched her trembling hands together, surprised when Sean put his hands over hers, channelling his calmness into her. 'You're an amazing woman and an amazing doctor, Jane.'

Jane nodded, unable to reply to his words.

'Ready?' he asked, and she could see the urgency in his eyes, his desperate need to get to the people who were in trouble and to help them. He wanted to help others, just as he'd been helping her by introducing her to Spencer and his family.

'Ready,' she confirmed.

His smile was bright and he winked at her before releasing her hands. 'Atta girl.' He turned and climbed from the car, retrieving his medical kit from the boot. 'I'm glad I had the presence of mind to shower and change before we left the beach,' he remarked when Jane came to stand next to him. He was pleased she was coming with him, pleased she was offering her expertise and proud that she was pushing through whatever mental blocks she still had about car accidents. Even though he'd watched her go incredibly pale, had seen the internal struggle within her, she was fighting past whatever barriers were in her way. She was doing what she knew in her heart was right. He took her hand in his. 'You're extraordinary, Jane Diamond.'

She opened her mouth to reply but no words came out. Speechless. He'd left her speechless with his lovely, heartfelt words. Sean believed in her.

Together, they made their way through the stopped traffic, hearing sirens in the distance. 'The accident couldn't have happened any longer than five minutes before we hit the gridlock,' Sean pointed out, and Jane noticed his tone was becoming more clipped, more detached, more professional.

She was the same usually, all brisk and professional... but not around car accidents. They were her weakness. However, she now had Sean to help provide her with the strength she needed and as they made their way briskly towards the wreckage, Jane tightened her grip on his fingers. He didn't pull away, didn't let her go, and as they came closer to where they could begin to see what had happened, Sean gave her hand a squeeze, stopping her for a moment.

'What is it?' she asked, her already heightened senses bringing worry into her tone.

'If you're not able to handle things, just tell me, Jane. Nothing wrong with that. Remember, I believe in you. You're far stronger than you think.' His words were soft yet still quick, as though he wanted to give her that final reassurance.

Jane stared into his eyes for what seemed an eternity yet was no more than a few seconds. 'I've got your back.' She nodded, realising that, no matter what they were about to face, she wasn't going to let Sean down.

'Let's do our jobs,' she said. He let go of her hand and led the way closer to where a few other people had climbed from their cars and were attempting to help out in whatever way they could.

'Two cars. No, three cars, but one is parked and empty,' Sean commented on first glance as he scanned the area. It appeared that one car and a mini-van with three occupants had crashed into the parked car. The other car had one occupant but the battered front windscreen and dented bonnet indicated that something had hit that car with force.

Jane scanned the area and it was then she saw the figure of an elderly man supine on the road.

'One patient on the road. Hit by car,' Jane said to Sean.

'The paramedics are almost through.' Sean pointed to where the ambulance was driving up the grassy median strip towards them. 'Do a quick triage on this patient, instruct the paramedics and find me.'

'OK.' Jane nodded and headed towards the man lying on the road, arriving a whole thirty seconds before one of the paramedics.

'I saw the whole thing,' one woman said. 'I was walking to my car and this man was just too slow crossing the road. It wasn't the driver's fault. He didn't see him until it was too late and then that other car swerved and—'

'Thank you,' Jane said. 'Please give him some room.' She quickly introduced herself to the paramedic while he opened the emergency medical kit for her. She pulled on a pair of gloves and addressed the patient. 'Can you hear me?' she said to the man. 'My name's Jane. I'm a doctor.'

'I can hear. I can hear,' the man returned.

'What's your name?' The man started to move but she quickly put her hand firmly on his shoulder, wanting to keep him still. 'Just stay there. It's all right.' Her tone was now calm and placating, needing him to understand but also to be reassured by her words. 'What's your name?' she asked again.

'Roderick.' His words were slightly slurred but she understood him.

'How old are you, Roderick?' the paramedic asked, as Jane started to feel bones, trying to ascertain if he'd broken anything.

'Eighty-five,' he slurred again.

'Have you been drinking, Roderick?'

'No, no drinking. My tongue.'

'Your tongue is sore?' she asked, as she checked his pulses, pleased there didn't seem to be any problem with his circulation.

'Yes.'

'You might have bitten it.'

'Too slow. I was too slow on the road.'

'No need to worry about that now,' she remarked. 'It feels as though you may have done some damage to your left leg but nothing that can't be fixed. I think you may have landed on your right wrist. Stay still, Roderick.'

The paramedic held Roderick's head still while Jane quickly looked at Roderick's tongue, listened to his breathing and ensured his pupils were equal and reacting to light. 'Stabilise and transfer,' she instructed the paramedics, feeling more comfortable with her role at the scene.

'Can you check out the driver of the car? He's over there.' She pointed to a man sitting on the grassy median strip, a few people gathered around him. 'I'll be over with the other patients in the mini-van.' Jane looked around for Sean but couldn't see him. The police and fire-brigade vehicles were making their way through, the police determined not only to assist with the accident but to get traffic sorted out as soon as possible. Good. At least that part of the accident scene was under control. Jane looked around for Sean, expecting to see him over at the mini-van, but he was nowhere in sight.

'Sean?' she called.

'Over here,' he replied, and Jane went up onto the footpath near the row of parked cars and it was then she saw him, attending to another person who was also lying on the ground. It was a woman of about twenty-two and she was clearly pregnant. 'Where did she come—?' As Jane asked the question she looked towards the road and it was then that she realised the mini-van's front windscreen was practically missing and that was because the young woman before her had gone all the way through it.

'She's been thrown from the car!' The words were a horrified whisper and when Jane closed her eyes she could see far too clearly, *feel* far too realistically the way the woman would have exited the car, head first, her face and arms scratched from the exploding glass, the dreaded sensation of being airborne and knowing there was nothing you could do to stop the impending pull of gravity as the ground loomed closer.

'Jane. *Jane.*'

Her eyes snapped open and she stared wild-eyed at Sean.

'Jane?' From her expression, Sean began to realise just what had happened to Jane in the car accident. 'You were thrown out,' he said softly, his words a statement of fact. He also knew that if he didn't manage to get Jane to focus on him rather than on the situation, she'd be of no use to him whatsoever and right now he really needed her assistance.

'Breathe, Jane. Breathe. Look into my eyes. Focus on my words.' He held her gaze, his words calm but firm. 'It's OK. You can do this. Just…breathe.'

Jane stared into his beautiful blue eyes, eyes that had often managed to turn her insides into mush, but this time they were silently telling her that he believed in her, that he needed her help and that she could get through this. He wouldn't leave her alone. He would be right beside her every step of the way and, to her utter amazement, she felt the panic and fear that had gripped her beginning to subside.

'That's it.' Sean glanced at his patient then back at her. 'Better?'

'Yes.'

'Good. This is Carly. She's twenty-two years old and thirty-three weeks pregnant. She's lying as still as possible, waiting for the next ambulance to make its way through.' Sean smiled down at the young woman, who seemed to relax a bit more beneath his soothing gaze. Jane couldn't blame her. Sean had a gorgeous smile and comforting eyes.

He lifted his head and looked at Jane again but this time something changed in his eyes. Worry. He was clearly worried and he wasn't worried for her but for Carly. This realisation helped Jane to take a deep breath and pull on her professionalism. If she could help Sean, if together they could help Carly, do everything they could to save this young woman's life, then she knew it was one enormous step towards healing the hurt she'd been carrying around for far too long.

Sean angled his head slightly, indicating he wanted her to come over and give him a second opinion on Carly's injuries. 'What's the situation? Police on the scene yet?' His tone was still calm and she picked up on the fact that he was trying not to scare or worry Carly too much, especially in her present condition.

'Just arrived. First ambulance is through. Paramedics attending.' She kept her words calm, logical, professional. Sean was right. She could do this. She stepped forward and reached into his medical kit, pulling on a pair of fresh gloves. 'Hi, Carly. I'm Jane. Just stay as still as possible.' She hoped her tone sounded reassuring and when she glanced at Sean and saw that proud smile on his face, her confidence soared.

'We have some cuts and abrasions to the legs and face.' Jane felt Carly's arms and checked her hands. 'Both wrists need splinting and possibly right elbow.' She took the stethoscope he proffered and listened to Carly's breathing. Then she pressed the stethoscope to Carly's abdomen and listened closely for ten seconds. She looked up, staring directly at Sean, realising that what she heard were the sounds of a baby going into distress. 'Carly, we need to check your blood pressure before we can get you stretchered up.'

Jane stood up and spotted a paramedic, carrying one of the usual large emergency kits they always used, heading in their direction. 'Over here,' she called, and within a moment the paramedic was putting a cervical collar around Carly's neck while Sean took Carly's blood pressure and Jane found an extra blanket.

'We need to put a blanket beneath her hip so we can keep the baby off the vena cava and stop the risk of deoxygenated blood.'

'Agreed.' Sean called over a few of the police officers to help.

When Carly was stabilised with her neck brace and a non-rebreather mask fitted over her mouth and nose, Sean put his hands on either side of Carly's head. 'On my command,' he said as the emergency workers and Jane got into position, 'we'll brace and roll.' Sean looked at the team before giving the command. With brisk but careful movements they rolled Carly to her side while Jane placed the blanket into position before Sean gave the command to roll Carly back.

'Carly, have you felt the baby kick since the accident?'

'Yes,' the frightened woman replied, her words a little muffled beneath her mask.

'That's very good news,' Jane reassured her. 'I'd just like to have another feel of the baby. OK?'

'Yes,' Carly said again.

Jane concentrated, carefully feeling around Carly's abdomen, visualising the different body parts of the baby, checking where they were. 'Head's definitely engaged,' she remarked a moment later.

'OK. I think we can get Carly stretchered up,' Sean said, 'then off to the hospital. I'll phone ahead and speak to the obstetric registrar.'

The paramedic nodded and started taking Carly's observations. Sean and Jane stood and ripped off their gloves, walking a little way away from their patient. 'The baby's not liking this at all,' Jane remarked.

'Carly's BP is not where I'd like.'

'We'll need to watch her,' she agreed. 'Perhaps get a cannula in now.'

'Good idea. We'll need to put it in her ankle as both wrists are fractured.'

They turned and went back to Carly, letting the paramedics know they needed that extra line in, just in case. Jane took Carly's blood pressure again and agreed with Sean's assessment that it was a little low. She assisted the paramedics as they shifted Carly to the stretcher, Jane once more doing obs and checking the portable baby sphygmomanometer, which showed Jane that the baby wasn't taking too kindly to what was happening to its mother.

When they had Carly safely in the ambulance, the paramedics doing observations once more, Jane inserted the cannula into Carly's ankle.

'I'm going to get an update on what's happening with Carly's friends in the mini-van,' Sean told her. 'She keeps asking and the information might help to settle her down if she knows her friends are all right.'

'Yes. Good thinking,' Jane replied, and pointed to a nearby police officer. Sean jogged over and spoke to the sergeant then headed back.

'Hi, Carly,' Sean said as he came into the ambulance and sat next to her. 'Your friends who were travelling with you are fine. The driver, Kieran, has a broken nose and a few cuts and bruises. The people in the back have seat-belt bruises and a bit of whiplash. That's it.'

Carly seemed to relax at this news, closing her eyes and breathing out with relief. 'They're OK,' she murmured.

'Let's monitor oxygen saturation and repeat fifteen-minute obs,' Jane instructed. 'I want to take a closer look at the baby.' She used an amplified stethoscope to obtain a more accurate reading of the baby's heartbeat, not liking what she heard. She felt the outside of Carly's abdomen and decided it might be best to do an internal.

'Carly, I'm going to need to check to see if you've started dilating.' There was no response from Carly and Jane called to her, 'Carly? Carly?'

'BP?' Sean asked, reaching for his stethoscope. He listened to her breathing.

'Dropping,' the paramedic replied.

'There's blood,' Jane remarked a second later. 'I think the uterus might have ruptured.'

'Push fluids,' Sean ordered. 'Carly? Can you hear me?' he asked, his tone firm and insistent.

'Baby's going into distress,' said Jane.

'Carly?'

'Mmm?' The tone was weak, as though Carly really didn't have the will to fight any more. 'Tired,' she mumbled.

'Come on, Carly. You've got a lot to live for. Are you having a boy or a girl? Do you know?'

'Boy,' she whispered.

'BP still dropping.'

'We need to get the baby out.'

'It hurts,' Carly complained, but at least her words were stronger.

'Carly, your uterus has ruptured. The baby is not doing

well. We need to get him out *now*. Do you understand?'
Jane asked, as she prepared the instruments she would
need.

'I'll organise an anaesthetic,' Sean stated and together
with the paramedic they began to get Carly organised.

'Carly, we need to get the baby out. If we don't, we risk
losing both of you. Do you understand?'

'Yes.'

Sean and the paramedic sedated Carly. 'Review BP,'
Sean requested.

The paramedic nodded, carrying out the instructions.
'Improving,' he remarked.

Jane looked to Sean. 'I'll deliver. You be ready to receive.'

'Agreed.'

It didn't take long for the administered anaesthetic to
take effect and soon Jane had the scalpel in hand and was
making an incision along the Caesarean line.

'I need more exposure. Retract,' Jane called, and Sean
duly inserted the retractors. 'Scalpel,' she said again, unable to believe the amount of blood. They worked seam-
lessly together as though they'd been doing it for years,
Sean able to pre-empt everything she required. 'Something
has definitely ruptured,' she remarked.

'We can keep her stable and once the baby's out you
can take a closer look around.'

'Agreed.' Jane concentrated on the present scenario,
visualising it in her mind before she reached in to grab
hold of the baby's head. She'd assisted with several Caesarean section births over the years but never in circumstances like this. Thankfully, they had a lot of equipment
in the ambulance but still she was having to improvise as
she went along. 'I've got him.' She kept a firm grip on the
little fellow and gently brought him out.

'BP steady and holding,' the paramedic reported.

'Ready and waiting,' Sean said, holding out a sterile towel ready to receive the baby.

'Out you come, mate,' she said, and in another moment Jane lifted the baby boy from his mother's womb and into Sean's large, capable hands beneath the sterile towel.

'Clamp and cut,' he instructed the paramedic, as Jane set about delivering the placenta. It was her job to look after the mother but she was acutely aware of the fact that the baby was not breathing.

'No tone. Bag him. Begin cardiac massage.' While Sean and one of the paramedics worked on the baby, she tried to focus her thoughts on discovering the source of the bleed.

'BP?' she asked, and the paramedic quickly took the observation.

'Steady.'

'Keep maintaining fluids. That's it, Carly. You stay with us,' she encouraged the unconscious mother. 'How's the baby doing?' Jane asked.

'Check pulse,' Sean said, and the paramedic pressed his fingers to the baby's groin, everyone silently praying the pulse was there.

'It's there! Faint but there.'

Jane breathed a heavy sigh of relief. 'He's a strong one.'

'He's still having a little difficulty breathing but he *is* breathing. We'll intubate and get this ambulance under way to the hospital.' Sean continued to attend to the baby and Jane continued to investigate the source of Carly's internal bleeding.

'Swab,' she instructed the paramedic who was assisting her. 'I need more light.' As she'd commanded, a strong beam of torchlight was directed where she needed it. 'Ah. There it is. Clamp.' She accepted the instrument and thankfully soon had the bleed under control. 'How's the baby?'

'Colour returning. Five minute APGAR is seven.'

'Excellent. Let's get moving.' And with Carly and the baby now in a more stable situation, one of the paramedics exited the back and headed around to the driver's seat, all of them thankful that the police had managed to control the traffic so the area wasn't as gridlocked.

It wasn't until they arrived at the hospital, the obstetric registrar and neonatal team waiting to take over, that Jane started to feel fatigue beginning to set in.

'Well, that wasn't the sort of ending I'd had planned for our day together,' Sean remarked after they'd cleaned up. They were in the A and E staffroom, Jane sipping the cup of relaxing tea Sean had made for her.

'What *did* you have in mind?' she asked, resting her head back against the wall, watching Sean through heavy-lidded eyes.

He shrugged and came over, sitting beside her and brushing her fringe from her eyes. 'A quiet chat, a nice cuppa.'

'Isn't that what we're doing now?' Jane couldn't disguise the huskiness in her tone and knew Sean was aware of it from the way he raised one eyebrow. That slow, irresistible smile started to appear on his lips. There was nothing she could do to control her emotions. She was exhausted, worn out, the emergency having zapped all her usual shields.

'Not exactly the venue I'd imagined but I guess so.' He brushed his fingers down her cheek, tenderly caressing her skin. 'Jane, you're tying me in knots. I can't seem to think straight when I'm around you and I can't seem to concentrate at all when we're apart.'

'I think you're exaggerating.'

His smile increased. 'Perhaps.' He brushed his thumb

over her lips, just as he'd done previously. 'You're remarkable. So strong and valiant.'

'I don't—'

'Shh. I'm trying to compliment you.'

'Oh. Sorry.' She was instantly contrite but somewhere, deep down inside her, she started to feel bold, started to feel that perhaps, with the way he was looking at her, with the way he seemed to be looking into her eyes as though she were the most precious person in the world to him, she might be able to take a chance. She gave him a little smile. 'I thought you might be wanting to kiss me.'

'Well...' His eyebrow rose in interest. 'That, too.' He swallowed and brushed his thumb once more over her lips, before edging back slightly to remove the teacup from her hands and place it on the table. He used the opportunity to move in even closer, leaning towards her, pleased when she didn't pull back but instead seemed to welcome his nearness. 'Is that what you want?'

'Yes. Yes, Sean, it is.' Her lips parted to allow the pent-up air to escape.

He exhaled slowly and came closer. 'Am I dreaming?' he whispered, his breath mingling with hers.

'If you are, then it's a dream we're sharing,' she returned, her tone equally as soft, equally as intimate.

'A shared dream,' he murmured, before his lips finally made contact with hers.

CHAPTER TEN

JANE COULDN'T BELIEVE the way it felt to be kissed by Sean. His mouth was gentle on her own, tenderly moving, testing, allowing her to pull away at any given moment, but that was the last thing she wanted. It was only now that she realised *this* was what she'd been yearning for for so long.

It wasn't just the fact that Sean wanted to kiss her but the fact that it was *Sean* kissing her. As though waiting for her to make the decision whether to pull away or to continue with this gloriousness, he pressed small butterfly kisses to her lips until Jane reached out to thread her fingers through his hair, encouraging him to stay as close to her as possible.

Even then, even after she'd put more urgency into her kiss, wanting to show him that without a shadow of a doubt she wanted this as well, Sean still hesitated, pulling back and opening his eyes to gaze down into her upturned face.

'Are you sure?' he whispered.

'Yes.'

'This could change…everything,' he murmured.

'Yes.' Her eyelids fluttered open and she gazed at him with desire in her eyes. Could he see the desire? Could he see just how much she wanted him? Needed him?

Unable to stop herself, she suddenly yawned and then smiled sheepishly at Sean. 'Sorry.'

He shook his head and brushed one last kiss across her mouth. 'It's my fault for not realising how exhausted you must be.'

'We helped out in the same emergency,' she pointed out, annoyed with herself for breaking the moment. 'Why aren't you tired?'

'You've faced far more than an emergency today. First meeting the rest of my family—'

'They're wonderful people, Sean. You're very lucky.'

'And if that wasn't nerve-racking enough, having to face the demons of your past, putting your own personal trauma aside in order to help out someone who was in a similar situation.'

'I couldn't have done it without you. You were my anchor,' she murmured, as he carefully removed her hands from his hair, entwining his fingers with hers.

'I'm thinking we're good together.' He gave her hands a little squeeze, before edging back and pulling her to her feet. 'I also think it's best if we get you back to the residential wing before you fall asleep right here in the staffroom.'

'If I did, would you be my knight in shining armour and carry me back to my castle?' The words were that of a constant fairy-tale, one which she'd dreamt of over the years, desperately hoping that one day she would meet the man who was able to see the *real* her, to want the *real* her, to love the *real* her. Was it possible that Sean was that man?

'Without a doubt,' he murmured, dropping a kiss to the tip of her nose before letting go of her hands in order to quickly tidy the staffroom, tossing out the remainder of their drinks and washing the cups.

'You're quite adept in the kitchen,' she remarked, when he linked his hand with hers and led them out into A and E.

He pointed to himself with his free hand. 'Single parent, remember? Adept at a lot of domestic duties.' He led her through A and E, completely oblivious to the curious glances they were receiving from a few of the staff because they were holding hands. Jane hated being the source of gossip, but at the moment she had to admit that she felt sort of…delighted that Sean wasn't afraid to show the world—or at least the A and E staff—that he cared for her. She only hoped she wasn't making a grave mistake.

She pushed the negative thought aside as they continued towards the residential wing, Sean continuing to hold firmly to her hand until they stood in the corridor outside her room.

He turned her to face him, quickly enveloping her in his arms and holding her close. 'Thank you for coming today.' His words were thick with repressed emotion and Jane received the distinct impression that although he wanted to come in with her, he was also leaving the decision up to her.

She swallowed. Could she do this? Could she let him in? Not only into her room but also into her heart? True, he was already there in an emotional sense but was it possible for her to let him see the *real* her? For him to see her scars? With Eamon, she'd been incredibly reserved, avoiding intimacy with him for as long as possible, until that one night when she'd made the mistake of opening up to him, showing him her scars and watching the revulsion cross his face.

She'd known, as soon as she'd witnessed his expression, that he would find some excuse to leave, find some reason for calling off their engagement, and forty-eight hours later that was exactly what had happened.

If things were going to progress with Sean, if there was any hope for any sort of future for them, then she preferred to know sooner rather than later. If she showed him her scars tonight, if she unveiled herself, she'd know as soon as he saw the deformity of her skin whether or not he truly cared about her. It was a risk but this way, if he did reject her, she'd be able to start the healing, start to find an even footing where she could quash the love she was beginning to feel for him and treat him as nothing more than a colleague and friend.

'The sooner the better,' she murmured against his chest.

'Hmm?' he asked, his big, strong arms still holding her close. Jane eased back and looked at him.

'Come in.'

Sean stared at her for a long moment as though she'd just spoken a foreign language and his sluggish mind was trying to translate. 'Wait. What?'

Jane fished around in her bag for her hospital lanyard, which held her room keycard, and quickly opened the room before she could change her mind. 'Come in,' she invited, holding the door for him.

'Jane? Are you sure? I mean...' He hesitated at the threshold. 'I want to... Don't get me wrong but—'

'Shh.' She quietened him, holding up one finger for silence. Then beckoned him forward and without another word from either of them Sean walked in, letting Jane close the door behind him. 'There's something I want to show you and I want to show you before I lose my nerve.'

'Jane?'

'I like you, Sean.' She pointed to the chair near the small breakfast table, indicating he should sit down.

'I like you, too, Jane.'

'OK.' She stepped forward after he'd sat down and pressed a finger to his lips. 'If this is going to work, I need you to be quiet.'

He frowned and whispered against her finger, his eyes filled with questions. 'If *what* is going to work?'

'Shh.' She bent her head and brushed a kiss across his

lips, before drawing in a deep breath and stepping away from him. 'This is important to me and…' She closed her eyes and started to unbutton her long-sleeved cotton shirt.

'Jane. No. Wait.' Sean shot to his feet.

Her eyes snapped open and she stared at him. 'What?'

'I don't think you should… I mean…just wait a minute and, uh…' He raked an unsteady hand through his hair, his confusion evident in his concerned blue gaze. 'I thought we could just talk and perhaps…well, if things escalated to that but…even then…' He stopped, belatedly realising he was beginning to trip over his words.

Jane was family. He'd invited her to become a part of his family so she wouldn't have to be alone any more, so that she could spend time with Spencer and finally feel that after all these years she was no longer alone, and while he was most definitely attracted to her, and had been pleasantly surprised when she'd taken charge just now, the last thing he'd expected from her was some sort of striptease! Was this how the men in her life had previously treated her? Like some sort of possession to do with as they wished? Did she consider only their pleasure but not her own?

He didn't treat women in this way. He'd been raised to respect women, to cherish them and to treat them as equals.

'I do want to talk,' she said, but that didn't stop her from unbuttoning her shirt. 'Please, sit down. I need to get through this now before…before…' She stopped, unable to voice the way she felt about him. It was definitely different from any other feelings she'd had in the past. Even with Eamon, the man she'd been about to marry, she hadn't felt so comfortable or accepted, but she knew if there was any hope of a future with Sean, any hope at all, she needed to be completely open and honest with him, and that meant showing him her hideous body.

'Please sit,' she urged again, and it was the hint of veiled desperation in her voice that made him do as she asked. He swallowed, watching her every move, and when she'd finished undoing all the buttons on the shirt, she took off her glasses and put them onto the table, the shirt still remaining closed.

'Today was difficult for me, in many ways. Meeting your family…' She smiled warmly at him as the memories of her wonderful time at the beach—feeling so included—washed over her. 'That has definitely been the highlight. But the accident, facing what had happened to me all those years ago, being in A and E—a department I avoid at all costs if possible—was…confronting.'

'You did so well, Ja—'

'Shh.' She spoke the sound softly before drawing in another breath and holding his gaze. 'I remember everything about the accident, every minute detail as though it happened only yesterday. I want to tell you, Sean. I want you to *know* me, the *real* me, and to do that I need to open myself, open my past up to you, to let you into my deepest, darkest secrets.'

Sean didn't speak this time but instead nodded once, wanting to convey to her that he now understood more of what she was trying to do…and he was incredibly impressed by her strength.

'We were driving home from a wedding, which had been up in the hills. I used to get carsick if I sat in the back so my mother had insisted that I sit in the front and she and Daina would sit in the back seat. Once we'd come down off the hills, the road now not so winding, Daina declared that it was her turn to sit in the front but my father refused to pull over. It had been raining, there was quite a bit of traffic on the road and he'd been drinking at the wedding. He was agitated and annoyed. He also had a very short fuse. My mother was trying to keep both Daina and my father under control by yelling at them to stop yelling at each other.

'Then Daina decided we could just switch places at the next red traffic light. It would have to be quick, she said. I was to climb into the back while she ran around the outside of the car. I didn't realise…' Jane stopped and swallowed over her dry mouth, her words still quiet and straightforward with only the mildest hint of disbelief '…until it was too late that she'd already unbuckled my seat belt. A dog ran onto the road, between our car and the car in front, and because of my dad's slower reflexes he swerved late and smashed our car into an enormous tree, as well as collecting a few other cars along the way.'

Jane wanted to close her eyes, to hide from him as she recalled the next bit, but if she did, she'd miss gauging Sean's reaction to her disfigured body. She didn't want to witness the repulsion she knew would come but if she didn't put herself through this now, it would only make it more difficult for her to get over him later.

She pursed her lips together and forced her breathing to remain calm as she continued. 'I felt as though I'd been sitting on an ejector seat. One moment I was looking back at Daina and the next I experienced searing pain as the windscreen glass cut into my face, arms and hands. I could see the ground beneath me, as though I was frozen in time, but it loomed closer and closer until I thudded down, skidding a little. The pain in my hands, my wrists was the first wave I felt. It was blindingly agonising and yet another pain made itself known.' She paused and gripped the edge of the shirt with both hands, slowly removing it to reveal the thin singlet top beneath.

She saw Sean's gaze dip to look at her arms, seeing the scars running up her arms. Would he realise that these scars were why she always wore long-sleeved tops and shirts? She heard his sharp intake of breath as she lifted the singlet top to reveal the large area around her side and abdomen, covered in scars and three different skin grafts.

'I landed on a large stick, which did quite a bit of internal damage.' She turned slightly so he could see the full effect. Her skin was disfigured and stretched, looking like a very bad patchwork quilt. 'I required kidney surgery and bowel surgery to fix the internal organs and then the skin grafts began, not all of them working the first time.' She twisted her shoulder to show him the ten-centimetre-long scar that had, over time, faded to become a paler shade of pink.

'Not only was I disfigured on the outside, I was broken on the inside. My parents died in that accident, my father of a fatal blow to the head and my mother bled out internally. And although they may not have been the best of parents, certainly having their fair share of problems, they were still my parents and I grieved deeply for them.'

Sean continued to stare at her, and she continued to carefully watch his expression. His brow was puckered in a slight frown but she hoped it was a frown of empathy rather than one of disgust. Was he looking at her with a clinical eye? Switching his mind from sensual mode to practical mode? Would he ever be able to regard her as a desirable woman? An object of beauty? A woman he wasn't too repulsed to touch and caress? Could he accept her? Would he ever tenderly caress and touch her badly stitched-together skin?

Jane held her breath, trying desperately to figure out what he was thinking. She simply stood there before him, not only baring her body but baring her soul. Couldn't he see how important this was to her? How she needed to be reassured? To be told that her life wasn't going to remain as lonely and as devoid of personal emotional connections as it had been for far too long? Was he the man who might love her as she hoped?

'I don't remember Daina having any scars.' His voice was deep yet distant and Jane's eyelids fluttered closed as horrified pain pierced her heart. She'd made another mistake. She'd opened up the box that contained her darkest fears and exposed herself to him…and all he could think about was Daina.

She worked hard to control the tears that were rising up within her, her head feeling incredibly heavy with the instant headache pounding against her temples. *You idiot. You stupid, disfigured nobody.* She couldn't stop the voice that penetrated her mind, the voice that always sounded exactly like Daina's. *Whatever made you think a man, especially one like Sean, so handsome and sexy, could love you?*

'Jane?'

She paused the voice in her head, knowing it would definitely continue later, and opened her eyes, glaring at him as she quickly pulled her clothes back over her body, turning her back to him as she attempted to button up her shirt, even though her trembling fingers made it nigh on impossible. She forced herself to concentrate on the menial task, to push away those other thoughts, to push away the answer to her initial question. Would Sean be able to accept her for who she was, scars and all? Clearly, he could not.

'She had bruises and cuts but they quickly disappeared,' Jane remarked woodenly. All she wanted now was for Sean to go, to leave her alone, to let her deal with the wounds he'd just inflicted. Why had she hoped for tender words? For a level of understanding about why she'd needed to literally bare her soul to him?

He was the same as all other men. More interested in

himself, his world, his life. Why had she thought he might be any different? Couldn't he see, didn't he understand that she needed reassurance? She knew she was broken but she wasn't relying on him to *fix* her, she was relying on him to accept her, to not care about Daina or any other woman, not here, not right now.

The first tear rolled down her cheek and she impatiently brushed it away. She didn't want to guilt Sean with her tears, to have him hold her, offering insincere comfort. Not now, not when he'd shown his true nature.

She must have stood there with her back to him for longer than she'd realised because when he spoke her name, she heard the questioning urgency in the tone.

'Jane?' He placed his hand on her shoulder but she shrugged away from his touch, not realising he'd moved from the chair. 'Jane, what is it?'

'What *is* it?' she asked, her words angry, her tears choking in her throat. She shook her head and sniffed, knowing she should get control over her emotions but realising she might have passed the point where logical thought was possible. 'How can you even ask me that? I...' She walked stiffly away from him, her movements stilted as though her brain was having difficulty sending signals to her limbs.

'I'm not sure I underst—'

'Of course you don't.' She rolled her eyes and shook her head. 'Why? Why did I even bother?' she whispered, more to herself than to him.

Sean stepped forward and placed both hands on her shoulders, wanting her to look at him. 'Jane?'

'Get your hands off me,' she growled, her voice low but steady. He gazed down into her face for a whole three seconds before doing as she'd asked. He stepped back and thrust both hands into his hair before placing them on his hips and looking at her as though she were a puzzle he simply couldn't figure out.

Jane drew in a breath, trying to muster as much civility as she could. The emotions were beginning to erupt and she knew of old that if she tried to quell them too much, it only made matters worse.

'I think you should leave.'

Sean shifted his stance, still staring at her in utter confusion. He opened his mouth to say something then closed it again before shaking his head. 'If that's what you want.'

'It is.'

'Then I'll go.'

Although he said the words, he still didn't move for a good ten seconds, the two of them standing there, staring at each other. There was no way she could decipher his expression and right now she was too distraught to care. The only thought that kept spinning around in her mind was that although she may have felt some sort of bond with Sean, although they may have acknowledged an attraction to each other, that attraction had abruptly come to an end the instant he'd seen her disfigurement.

He nodded and shoved his hands into his pockets. 'I'll go.'

With that, he walked past her to the door and without looking back opened it and left.

As the door slowly closed behind him, the rush of pain, anguish and loneliness, all the emotions she'd been fighting for far too long, washed over her like a raging torrent, flooding her mind. With her legs no longer able to support her, she crumpled to the floor as the first sobs of heartbreak began to rack her body.

Despite the way Sean loved his family, despite the way he loved his son, there was no denying the fact that he could never love a freak like her.

CHAPTER ELEVEN

FOR THE NEXT three days Sean had the distinct impression that Jane was doing her best to avoid him. Initially he'd thought she was embarrassed at having shown him her body, that she needed some time to come to terms with her vulnerability, but every time he walked onto the ward, she would leave at her earliest convenience, not even bothering to utter an excuse.

He knew she'd been to Maternity to check on both Carly and the baby because when he'd gone to see how mother and baby were doing, Carly had sung Jane's praises, letting Sean know how wonderful she was.

'She told me that when she was a teenager she was also in a car accident like me. She opened up to me, she told me she knew *exactly* what I was feeling and why it was important for me to speak to a psychologist about it now, rather than letting the emotions build up and get the better of me.'

'Wise words,' Sean had remarked, already having read in Carly's file that she'd bluntly refused to see the psychologist.

'I can't believe she opened up to me like she did. She didn't have to but because she did I can see that she's not just spouting hospital rules at me but that she really does care because she *understands*.'

'Yes.' Sean knew Carly wasn't the only patient to be saying such things about the wonderful Jane Diamond. Tessa, who was beginning to show definite signs of improvement as far as her eating habits went, continued to be glued to Jane's side as much as possible. He'd read in Tessa's notes that Jane had sat in on every counselling session with the parents, offering helpful suggestions as to ways they could support both their daughters—the one who was bullying and the one who was being bullied.

Jane had also dropped around to spend some time with Spencer, or so his mother had told him late yesterday evening. Sean found it interesting that Jane had chosen to see her nephew on the evening when she knew he'd be in departmental meetings. In fact, it seemed that Jane had time for everyone…except him.

Perhaps the kisses they'd shared had been enough to scare her off? Perhaps she now wanted to just be friends and not be romantically involved…but if that was the case, why had she shown him her scars in the first place? He couldn't believe how amazing she was, how brave and incredibly beautiful, and now she seemed to want nothing to do with him.

He'd left her messages on her phone. Some jokingly jovial, telling her he couldn't sleep and needed her to sing him a lullaby over the phone, and when she hadn't returned any of his calls he'd left messages that were filled with concern and confusion. No reply.

He still wanted to pursue the attraction he felt for her, to figure out what had gone wrong and why she was bent on avoiding him. He knew she felt the same way, too, or at least she had. So why had she shut him out? What had he done? Said? He was at a loss to figure it out and it had been constantly at the back of his mind for the past three days, ever since she'd asked him to leave her room.

Sean flicked back the bed sheet and stalked from his bedroom, deciding it was better to give up on attempts to sleep and try and catch up on some paperwork. 'At least the bureaucracy of the hospital will help get your mind off Jane,' he murmured as he made himself a cup of tea.

He worked solidly for half an hour, the light over his paper-strewn dining-room table sufficiently illuminating the area as the clock in the hallway ticked steadily towards dawn.

'Sean?'

He heard his mother's voice at the top of the stairs. 'Are you awake?'

'Mum? Come on down.'

Louise did as he asked, coming into the room, her summer dressing gown pulled tight around her. 'Can't sleep either?' she asked rhetorically. Sean's answer was a shrug of his shoulders. 'Problem at the hospital?'

'Not really.'

'Problem with Spencer?'

'No. He's fine.'

Louise settled herself at the table and looked closely at her son for a moment. 'Problem with...Jane?'

Sean eyed his mother cautiously. 'What makes you ask that?'

'Oh, I don't know. When she was here she kept changing the subject every time I mentioned your name.'

Sean put his pen down and groaned, resting his head in his hands. So she really was avoiding him, not just being super-busy and efficient at work. He'd hoped it was the latter, he'd hoped he was reading the signals incorrectly, but if his mother had picked up on something—and she was usually incredibly astute—then there was definitely something wrong.

'I thought the two of you were getting along very well,'

Louise stated. 'It certainly looked that way when we were at the beach.'

'The beach.' He lifted his head from his hands. 'That seems so long ago now.'

'I'm sorry if you think I'm prying, son, but how *do* you feel about Jane? Tell me to shut up and mind my own business if you want but I only ask because I care about you, and about Jane and about Spencer. Whether you like it or not, your son became very much involved in all of this the instant you gave Jane access to him.'

'You think I should have kept her away?'

'No. Heavens, no. From what I can observe, Jane hasn't had the easiest of lives and it's a credit to her that she's such a strong survivor.'

'Yes.' Sean thought back to the way she'd bravely revealed her scars to him, the way her big eyes had been wide with fear, like a scared little rabbit, and yet she'd done it. She'd conquered her fear and shown him her deepest, darkest secret and then…

'It's as though she sometimes gets swamped with the emotions from her past,' he said out loud, standing and pacing the room. 'I thought she was steering clear of me because she…well, she opened up to me.' He stopped pacing and raked a hand through his hair. 'But if she was avoiding talking about me, then it must have been… But what did I do?'

'How did she open up to you?' Louise asked.

Sean looked at the floor then met his mother's eyes. 'She showed me her scars.'

'From the car accident when she was a teenager? The one where her parents died?'

'Yes.' He shook his head. 'What she must have endured.'

'And what did you say?'

'Huh?'

'After she'd bared her soul to you—because that's what she was doing, darling—what did you say?'

Sean frowned. 'I didn't…say…' He tried to recollect what had happened next. 'She showed me her scars, she told me her parents had died in that accident. I was surprised that Daina hadn't been scarred in any way, given the severity of the accident.'

Louise gaped at her son. 'Tell me you didn't mention Daina.'

'What? I just said I didn't remember Daina being scar—' He stopped talking and closed his eyes, slowly shaking his head from side to side. 'She thought I was comparing them. Her and Daina.' And that had been when she'd turned away from him, that had been when she'd finally stared at him with the eyes of a stranger and told him to leave. He'd only done as she asked because he'd thought it had all been too much for her and that she wanted to be alone.

'Has Jane ever had a serious relationship before?'

'Yes.' The answer was a whisper as he quickly recalled what she'd told him. 'She said he broke off the engagement because she kept herself hidden, that she was secretive, and that in the end she wasn't the woman he wanted.' Regret pierced Sean's soul at the thought of the pain he'd caused Jane.

If she was under the impression that he thought her scars ugly and disfiguring then he had to change her mind. He had to show her that she'd become important to him, that she'd somehow managed to open his heart, helped him to heal from his past pain and to risk loving again.

'Loving?' His eyes widened as the word tripped off his tongue. He glanced at his mother to find her watching him intently.

'I don't know what just went on inside your head, son.'

She chuckled as she stood and tightened the belt of her dressing gown. 'But it was funny watching a multitude of emotions work their way across your face.' She leaned up and pressed a kiss to his cheek. 'Let me know if your father or I can be of any help.'

'Can you look after Spencer when he wakes up in about half an hour?' Sean's mind was working at a rate of knots. 'I need to fix this. I need to let Jane know that's not how things are, that's not how I feel, and I think I know exactly how to accomplish that.'

Louise nodded. 'I'm still only getting half the picture but that's all right. I'll wait until the ending's written.' She pointed a finger at him, her tone filled with mock warning. 'Just make it a happy one.'

As Louise headed back up the stairs, yawning as she went, Sean looked at the clock on the wall. 'Half past five.' He walked to his phone, his gut telling him that Jane would not be asleep, that she'd no doubt be somewhere in the ward, helping her patients through the night. 'Anthea?' he said when the phone on the ward was answered. 'It's Sean. Is Jane on the ward?'

'Yes, she is. Do you want me to get her for you?'

'Er…no. No. It's fine.' He was about to say goodbye but added quickly, 'Don't tell her I called. OK?'

'OK.'

'And if possible, can you keep her on the ward until I get there? Shouldn't be more than half an hour or so.'

'OK,' Anthea said again, her tone a little curious. 'Are you feeling all right, Sean?'

Sean grinned as his plan began to solidify. 'Anthea, I've never been better in my life!'

Jane sat by Tessa's bedside, pleased with the progress the young girl had made over the past few weeks. It made her feel wonderful to be able to help someone because it was a small way of righting the wrongs that had been done to her. Tessa was due to be discharged tomorrow and was naturally apprehensive at going home.

'I'm safe here. Why can't I stay here?' she'd asked Jane only a few hours ago, the rest of the ward quiet as the two of them had talked softly.

'Because you need to grow stronger at home. Staying here will do nothing for you, Tessa. Facing your darkest fears is...' Jane had stopped, as the image of Sean's gaze on her disfigured body, the look of disbelief in his eyes, had come immediately to mind. She'd pushed it aside. 'Is how you become strong. Your parents know what your sister was doing to you and they've been able to find out what was wrong with your sister, why she felt it necessary to bully you.'

'But what about you?' Tessa had held Jane's hand. 'Will I see you again?'

'You're seeing me in three days' time in my clinic.'

Tessa had looked at Jane then, caution entering her eyes. 'Are you for real or are you just being my doctor?' Blunt and to the point. Jane's smile had been bright because two weeks ago Tessa wouldn't have had the courage to ask such a thing.

'I'm both. I'm your doctor first and foremost but I'm also your friend.'

'So we can, you know, go the park one day or something like that?'

'What about the movies?' Jane had suggested, and Tessa's eyes had brightened with absolute delight.

'Really?'

'Of course.' Jane had laughed at the reaction and Tessa had joined in before sighing as though a huge weight had just been removed from her shoulders. Fifteen minutes later, the child had drifted off into a calm and comfort-able sleep.

Jane sat there, envying the little girl. Yes, things had been bad but Tessa was getting help and, most importantly, was responding to that help. If only her own life could be as easily fixed, but that wasn't to be. She had to somehow figure out a way to endure working alongside the man who had stolen her heart but rejected her body.

Closing her eyes, she couldn't help but remember the way he'd held her so tenderly, the way he'd kissed her, mur-mured that he thought her beautiful. If only it had been true. At least she'd found out early on, at least she hadn't spent months of her time here in Adelaide fixating on the hope that something might happen between Sean and her-self. The fact that he'd generously included her in his fam-ily circle, allowing her access to Spencer, was something she would be forever grateful for, and where she'd thought he'd accepted her for who she was, that he might be able to see past the scars on her body to the real her, cowering inside…well, she'd been mistaken before and she shouldn't have been surprised that it had happened again.

Realising if she sat here allowing her thoughts to con-tinue in this manner, she'd probably end up bursting into tears and waking Tessa, she uncurled herself from the chair. Quietly standing up and heading to the nurses' sta-tion, she found Anthea busy filling in paperwork, getting ready for the hand-over.

It was just after six o'clock in the morning and while Jane had managed a few hours' sleep prior to coming and checking on Tessa, she was starting to feel fatigued. Even if she wanted to sleep, she knew as soon as her eyes closed, all she would see would be Sean's grim face, his eyebrows drawn together as he stared at her grotesque body.

'Not a bad night,' Anthea murmured, then gestured in

Tessa's direction. 'Is she anxious about going home this morning?'

'Yes. Listen, I might head back to my room, shower, change, have something to eat and then be back here in time for her nine o'clock discharge.'

'Uh…sure, Jane, but, uh…would you mind just having a quick look at these files for me, please? I'm not sure if the medication dosages are correct.'

Jane sighed and nodded. 'Sure.' She accepted the files from Anthea, noticing the other woman kept checking the clock on the wall and then glancing over Jane's shoulder towards the doors to the ward. 'Something wrong?' Jane asked ten minutes later.

'What? Oh. Uh. No.' Anthea shifted uncomfortably and couldn't help glancing at the clock once more.

'These dosages look fine.'

'Great. Good. Thanks.' Anthea glanced frantically around the nurses' station as though looking for something. 'Uh, actually, I can't…er…find…Tessa's discharge forms. Have they been prepared?'

'I filled in all the preliminary details only a few hours ago. They should be in her notes.' Jane went over to where the casenotes were kept and was surprised when she couldn't find Tessa's notes. 'They were right here.'

'Oh. I'll help you look for them,' Anthea quickly volunteered, once more glancing at the clock and then the doors to the ward. Jane frowned but decided that perhaps the fatigue of working through the night was starting to get to Anthea. Jane looked around the place and eventually found the notes under a different pile of papers, not at all where they should have been.

'Here they are.' She opened the notes and checked the discharge papers were in there. 'There you go.'

'Oh. Thanks. One of the enrolled nurses must have

moved them. Thanks, Jane.' There was a look of concern on Anthea's face.

'Are you sure you're all right? You're acting a little… strangely.'

Anthea laughed nervously. 'I'm just no good at this.'

A prickle of apprehension worked its way down Jane's back. 'No good at what?' she asked cautiously.

At that moment the ward doors opened and Anthea breathed a sigh of relief. 'Stalling,' the ward sister replied, before pointing.

Jane turned around slowly, sensing before she saw him that Sean had just entered the ward. Why had Anthea been stalling? Had Sean realised she'd been doing her best to avoid him? Had he employed the help of the ward sister in order to make her feel even more uncomfortable than she did? What had he told Anthea? Did the entire ward know about her scarred body?

The questions flooded her mind, one tripping over the other, her breathing becoming uneasy. She quickly looked behind Sean at the closing ward doors, wondering if there was any way she could escape, but with Anthea behind her and Sean walking towards her it appeared she was trapped.

Jane immediately pulled her sleeves down, then crossed her arms over her chest and lifted her chin, her eyes flashing defiantly. If she was going to be cornered, she was going to do her best to project an attitude of defensive fake nonchalance.

Sean took one look at her then glanced past her to Anthea. 'Thanks,' he remarked, which only made Jane more annoyed.

'What do you want, Sean?' she asked, completely failing to keep her emotions under control, her tone laced with annoyance.

'I want you.'

Her eyes opened wide at his words. 'Pardon?'

'I want you to come with me. Please.' He held out his hand, waiting for her to put hers into it. Instead, Jane shook her head and stepped around him, stalking out of the ward, hoping against hope that he wouldn't follow her.

'Jane.' He was closer than she'd realised and fell into step beside her. Thankfully he didn't try to stop her as she made her way through the hospital corridors, heading towards the residential wing. 'I'm sorry.'

'Sorry? About what?' Again, she hadn't managed to keep her tone absolutely devoid of emotion and she silently berated herself. She needed to get control over her emotions, not remember the way his big strong arms had held her, his fingers had caressed her, his lips had brushed tenderly and provocatively over her lips. She was not in love with him. She was *not*. She had to keep telling herself that because right now she knew it was an absolute lie.

'About walking out the door the other night.'

Jane faltered for a moment and Sean took the opportunity to place his hand on her arm and stop her in her tracks. 'Please, Jane. Just hear me out. If you want nothing to do with me after that, I promise I'll leave you alone.'

'Will you? Really?' She gazed up into his eyes, stunned and amazed to find him looking not only desperate but extremely contrite.

'Probably not.' He smiled and shrugged his shoulders. 'It's difficult for a man to leave the woman he's in love with, even if it's what she wants.'

Jane's throat went dry and she tried to swallow. 'Love?' she squeaked.

'Yes, Jane. I love you.' The words came easily to his lips and where he'd practised long and convincing speeches on the drive to the hospital, all that mattered right now was that she understood exactly how he felt. He tugged her into a small nook, out of the way of the main corridor, for a bit of privacy. 'I *love* you,' he repeated, emphasising the middle word. 'You've managed to unlock the pain from my past and make it disappear as if by magic. You've shown me I'm not only capable of trusting again but also of loving. You've been so incredibly brave, opening your heart to me, showing me your scars, and I...' He looked down into her face, overcome with love at her inner strength.

'It's all right, Sean.' She hung her head, her long hair hanging like a veil around her. 'I know my skin is grotes—'

'What? No. No.' He shook his head and lifted her chin so he could once more look into her eyes. 'You misunderstand me. I don't find your scars horrible or ugly or anything like that.'

'But...' Jane was unable to believe and accept what he was saying. 'You found me distasteful and...compared me to...to...'

'I'm sorry you took it that way. I wasn't comparing you to Daina. I was...astounded that she'd walked away with nothing and that you, so strong and so brave, had lost everything. She was... Her behaviour towards you was...' He shook his head. 'I don't want to talk about the past, about Daina. It's over and done with and there's nothing we can do to change it. What we *can* do is to move forward with our lives...together.' He took her hands in his and held them tightly.

'Sean?' His name was a whispered caress on her lips and in another moment he'd dipped his head and was brushing the sweetest of sweet kisses to her mouth.

'I love you, Jane. Scars and all.'

'But—'

'No buts. I love you, Jane. *Scars and all.*'

Tears instantly sprang to her eyes as she desperately

tried to accept what he was saying. She bit her lip but the action only caused him to kiss her once more.

'I love you, Jane, scars and all. And I am going to keep telling you that until you believe me. I love you, Jane. Scars and all.'

'Oh, Sean. Really?'

He smiled. 'I love you, Jane. Scars and all.' With that, she leaned into him and he immediately put his arms around her, drawing her close. 'Now, I have something special planned for us this morning.'

'You do?'

'Yes.' He looked down at her, unable to resist brushing another kiss to her lips. 'So would you do me the honour of trusting me? Of not asking too many questions and allowing me to follow through with my initial plan?'

'You have a plan?'

'Yes, but somehow, where you're concerned, they never seem to work out exactly as I imagined.'

'Why is that, do you think?' Jane reached out and brushed her fingers through his hair, delighted that she had the right to touch him. He loved her. Sean loved her—*scars and all.*

'Because you twist me into knots and no one's ever been able to do that before.'

Jane looked at him with a hint of doubt still in her eyes.

'No one,' he emphasised. 'You don't react the way women usually do. You march to the beat of your own drum and I adore that. You are unique, Jane.' He brushed the hair from her eyes and bent to kiss her lips once more. 'And you're doing it again. You're derailing me from the plans I have by being so incredibly wonderful.'

'And what are these "plans" that you have?'

'I want to take you back to my house so you can have breakfast with Spencer and me, so I can have the perfect setting where I can get down on one knee and ask you to become my wife.'

'Wife?' she squeaked.

'I love you, Jane. Why wouldn't I want to marry you?'

'But…I… Are you sure?'

'Never been surer of anything in my life.' Sean took her scarred arm in his hand, gently pushing up the sleeve. Next he brushed kisses up the length of her scar, wanting her to know that, beyond a doubt, he wanted her, needed her, loved her. He didn't care that she was scarred. The realisation made her feel foolish for having read his expression incorrectly the other night.

'Oh, Sean.' She shook her head. 'I'm sorry.'

'Sorry?' He met her gaze.

'Sorry for making you leave the other night. I thought you were disgusted by my scars, I thought you were like… other people.'

'Your former fiancé may not have been able to see past the physical to the stunningly beautiful woman that you really are—inside and out, as far as I'm concerned,' he quickly clarified, lest she take his words in the wrong way. 'But I'm not him. I love you, Jane. Scars and all.'

She nodded, starting to accept that what he said was the truth. He'd professed his love for her, he'd told her he wanted to propose to her, that he wanted her for his wife, and yet hadn't pressured her for any type of answer… giving her time to process and to think things over. Perhaps Sean did understand her, better than she understood herself.

'I…er…need to be back at the hospital by nine, so I can be here for Tessa's discharge,' she said, by way of explanation.

'Then we'd best get moving,' he told her, bending to kiss her lips again before slipping an arm about her waist and walking through the hospital, once more not caring who saw them or the tongues they set wagging.

During the drive to his house Sean chatted easily with her, as though it was quite normal for him to have professed his love for her, while she couldn't help feeling more and more nervous the closer they drew to his home.

'What if Spencer doesn't like me enough to have me for a stepmother?' Jane blurted out the instant he pulled into the driveway. 'I mean, he barely knows me and...isn't this all moving a bit too fast?'

Sean removed the key from the ignition, before unbuckling his seat belt and turning to face her.

'Jane. For a start, Spencer hasn't stopped talking about you since he met you.'

'He hasn't?'

'He thinks you're fantastic.'

'He does?'

'And, besides, it's clear to me—and to anyone who's seen you with him—just how much you care about him, how much you love him.'

'I do. He's the reason I came back to Adelaide.'

Sean took her hand in his and kissed it then instructed, 'Wait there.'

'Why?'

His smile broadened. 'I want to be chivalrous. Is that OK?'

'Oh. Uh...sure.' And so she sat in her seat, waiting for him to come around the car and open the door for her. Although the sun had only been up a short while, the heat was starting to make itself known, but it was nothing compared to the way Sean warmed her through and through when he smiled lovingly down at her.

'You still have your seat belt on,' he murmured when she looked up at him. 'Allow me.' He instantly leaned into the car, his face coming incredibly close to hers, his breath mingling with hers as he reached across to unclip the belt.

'Mmm,' he murmured, as he took the opportunity to press a few kisses to her cheek, Jane delighting in his tender touch. She angled her head so their lips could meet and when they did, with her finally starting to accept that he truly did love her, that he wanted to spend the rest of his life with her, that all her dreams did actually seem to be coming true, Jane kissed him back with all the love in her heart.

'Sean?' she murmured, caressing his face with her fingertips.

'Yes, my love?'

'I want you to know…that I don't like long engagements.'

At her words, a slow smile spread across his face. 'Duly noted.' He kissed her again, before helping her from the car and slipping his arms about her waist. 'I take it that your answer to my impending proposal will be yes?'

'How could you doubt it? Before I met you—this time around…' she quickly clarified, and he nodded, indicating he understood what it was she was saying. 'My life was… hollow. I'd look in the mirror and not recognise myself because I never really smiled any more. Sure, I'd smile for my patients, doing everything I could to help them. I'd smile for my colleagues, wanting to show that I could work alongside them, but I wasn't smiling for *me*.

'I guess, given my upbringing, that doing things for myself, rewarding myself, being kind to myself, wasn't something I'd ever thought possible. But now, thanks to you and your generosity in allowing me to become a part of your family, I no longer feel faceless or hollow. I can keep on living my life, surviving in the world I've built for myself, but…I don't want to.'

She placed both her hands to his face and looked directly into his eyes, his beautiful, blue hypnotic eyes. 'I want to be with you, Sean. With you and Spencer. I want to become a family. The three of us. I…I…' She stopped and sighed heavily.

'It's OK if you're not ready to say it, Jane. I don't need the words because I can see it in your eyes and, really, the other night you said all that needed to be said—I just didn't realise it. You bared your soul to me, you allowed me into your deepest, darkest secret and I am not only honoured, I'm humbled by it.' With that, he released her from his hold, took her hands in his and went down on one knee.

'This still isn't the way I'd planned to propose but it doesn't matter. It's the *right* time to ask you and believe me when I say, Jane—to me, you are perfect. In every way. Please, my love, consent to be my wife and Spencer's mother?'

'Oh, Sean,' she gasped, quickly tugging him to his feet. 'Yes.' She rose up on tiptoe and placed a kiss firmly to his mouth. 'Yes. Yes and yes again. You can propose to me as many times as you like and I will always say yes.'

Sean gathered her close, dipping his head down to claim her lips. 'I might just hold you to that.'

No sooner had he pressed his mouth to hers than they heard the front door open and Spencer came running out.

'Aunty Jane. Aunty Jane. You're here!'

Sean released Jane to briefly scoop his son into his arms. They looked across to the doorway where Louise was standing, dabbing at her eyes with a handkerchief, a big, bright smile on her face.

'Have you come for breakfast, Aunty Jane? There's a huge feast on the table inside and Grandma said I wasn't allow to touch *any* of it until you got home—but I sneaked a strawberry when she wasn't looking,' he confided in a stage whisper.

Jane couldn't help but laugh, unable to believe how happy she was.

'Shall we go in?' Sean asked Jane as he let the wriggling Spencer go, securing his arm around Jane's waist once more.

'Yes, *my love*, we shall.'

CHAPTER TWELVE

DURING THE NEXT few weeks after she'd accepted Sean's proposal Jane couldn't believe how happily her life had turned out. Not only had Louise and Barney well and truly accepted her as part of their family but they'd asked her to move into their guest room.

'Just until the wedding,' Louise had stated. 'That way, you'll be close to Sean and Spencer.' This arrangement suited Jane down to the ground as she wasn't used to making life-changing decisions in a rush.

'You could just sneak downstairs and stay with me,' Sean had said temptingly on more than one occasion, but he'd also understood Jane's need to take things slowly.

'Falling in love with you in such a short time has been enough of an emotional education,' she'd told him, before kissing him with all the love in her heart. 'Slowing things down isn't a bad idea, Sean. For all of us.'

'I know,' he'd agreed, but he had held her close while they'd waited for Spencer to finish getting ready for bed. 'I just never thought I'd feel this way, so...content. I want you, Jane. I want you to be my wife and I want it soon. Although things have happened faster than either of us probably imagined, it also feels so incredibly right. You said you don't like long engagements and neither do I.'

'But Spencer…'

'Feels the same way. He's already started calling you "Mum".'

Jane grinned widely; her heart burst with love every time Spencer did so. 'I never knew it would feel so…perfect.'

'We *are* perfect. The three of us.'

'I know but just the thought of organising a wedding, of actually setting a date—' She stopped. 'Sean, every time I've tried to make arrangements in the past, things have always gone wrong.'

He'd pondered her words for a moment before asking, 'What if I surprise you?'

'Surprise me?'

'Surprise wedding.'

'What? Like a surprise party?'

'Why not? That way you don't have to be stressed about it at all.'

She looked at him with surprise. 'You never fail to amaze me.' She kissed him quickly yet lovingly. 'Promise me you won't ever stop.'

'So I can organise a surprise wedding for you?'

'Um…' It would stop her from worrying and stressing about things. 'Are you sure you want to do it?'

Sean's answer had been to capture her mouth with his own. 'Absolutely.'

And so for the next few weeks, Jane simply released all that extra tension from her shoulders, amazed at how wonderful it was to have someone else to care about her burdens. What she *was* able to focus on was helping Louise plan Spencer's seventh birthday party.

'I know you wanted all the attention to be on Spencer and not on you, but I'm glad you're letting us make this a combined birthday party,' Louise said the day before the event as Jane helped her to put the finishing touches on Spencer's character birthday cake. She'd never made a birthday cake before, and certainly not one for the little boy who now called her Mummy.

'Spencer insisted. He said he wouldn't have a party at all if I didn't agree to have one with him.' Jane laughed as she licked a bit of the icing from the knife before putting the mixing bowls into the sink. 'He's so excited to be sharing his birthday with me. He told me it's our special bond.' And on hearing those words from the almost-seven-year-old, Jane had let go of the last tie she'd been holding onto from her past. No longer was Spencer her sister's son; instead, he was her birthday buddy. 'He's quite a charmer—just like his father.'

'It's hereditary,' Louise agreed, then glanced at the clock behind her. 'Good heavens. Is that the time?'

'Oh, I need to go and pick Spencer up from school,' Jane said, glad Sean had insisted she take a few days' annual leave before the birthday party.

'You'll enjoy the build-up to the party even more if you're not having to stress about patients and rush around at the hospital,' he'd said, and Jane had to admit he'd been right.

When Spencer got into the car, he was buzzing with delight about his party tomorrow.

'And we can't wait to go laser tagging and we've already decided who's going to be on my team and who is going to be on Tessa's team,' Spencer remarked.

'Tessa's looking forward to it, then?' It had only been after Tessa's discharge from the hospital that Jane had learned the little girl not only went to the same school as Spencer but was in his class. In true Booke family fashion, and without any prompting from the adults, Spencer had sought Tessa out, befriending her, and when Jane had seen the girl only a few days ago she'd been amazed at the transformation. A rosy glow had infused Tessa's cheeks and the smile on her face as she'd chatted animatedly with Spencer had filled Jane's heart with joy. 'These Booke men are quite wonderful,' she murmured.

'What did you say, Mummy?' Spencer asked.

Jane smiled at him. 'I said you and your dad are quite wonderful.'

'What does wonderful mean?' He tipped his head to the side and looked at her intently, as though he completely trusted her to know all the answers.

'Uh…' Jane thought for a moment. 'It means purple and green together,' she told him.

'Ohhh. Yeah. I get it now.' Spencer paused for one quick breath before continuing with what he'd been saying. 'And anyway Tessa and I both wanted you on our team but she said that as you were my new mother that you could be on my team. I can't wait until we have the cake. Is it finished? Did you and Grandma finish it?'

Jane laughed at the way he wasn't to be derailed from the topic at hand and listened intently as she drove them home in her new car. Home. How perfect that word sounded. True to his word, Sean hadn't said anything more to her about the wedding but when he'd asked her if she wanted to wear an engagement ring, Jane had shrugged.

'Not really. I mean, nine times out of ten I can't wear rings at the hospital so I don't see the point.'

'Were you always this practical?' he'd asked, with a wide smile on his face.

'I had to be.'

'And rightly so.' Sean had also had the impression that Jane didn't want the traditional wedding service with all the trappings and trimmings because that was exactly the wedding he'd had with Daina. If Daina had been a

Bridezilla, then Jane was the complete opposite. It was one of the reasons he loved her so much. She was simply perfect for him. 'Well…' he'd said a moment later, having thought about it. 'How about we have your wedding ring made up with a few diamonds inset?'

'I guess so but I'm not really a diamond sort of girl. I guess having a surname like Diamond all these years has put me off. However, I do like the idea of getting some stones inset. What's your birth stone?'

'I believe it's tanzanite.'

'And Spencer and I are both aquamarine so why not have a piece of tanzanite inset with an emerald either side? One for each of us.'

'And if we happen to blessed with more children in the future?'

Jane had glanced over at him, realising this was his way of asking her if she wanted children. She'd smiled reassuringly and nodded. 'Then I'll have to get the ring adjusted.'

Sean had reached over and kissed her hand. 'Sounds perfect.' He'd then told her he'd need her ring size and once that had been achieved, she'd gone back to simply enjoying her new world, the world of love and laughter and family. She'd been able to get to know Kathleen and Rosie much better and was enjoying playing a nightly game of chess with Barney. She really was part of the Booke family and when Sean came home from work that night she couldn't help but slip her arms about his waist and tell him just how much she loved being with him, being a part of his family.

Sean kissed her as though he hadn't seen her for weeks, rather than only since that morning. 'And tonight, my gorgeous Jane, I'm going to take you out for a special pre-birthday dinner because, believe me, although Spencer says he's happy to share his birthday with you, the day will still be all about him.'

'And I'm more than happy to have that happen.' She laughed.

'Go on up and get dressed. We have reservations in an hour.'

'Oh. Is it a fancy place? I'm not sure I have anything suitable to wear.'

'It's all taken care of.' He smiled and kissed her again. 'I love you, Jane. Every single part of you.'

'I believe you, Sean. I really do.' It was a few more minutes before she was able to head up to her room, excited that she was getting to enjoy a special, secret dinner for her birthday *just* with Sean.

On the bed, she found a garment bag and when she unzipped it, inside was the most wonderful cream-coloured dress she'd ever seen in her life. Simple in design, the straight skirt came to mid-calf while the bodice had small daisy flowers embroidered around the waist and a scooped neckline. The dress was sleeveless but also in the garment bag was a light shawl, embroidered with daisies. She stared at the dress for a whole minute, unable to believe something so beautiful was being given to her.

At the knock on her door, she jumped. 'It's only me,' Louise called, opening the door a little. 'Sean told me he's taking you out for a special dinner. Can I come in?'

'Look what Sean bought me!' Jane pointed to the dress as Louise came into the room, closing the door behind her.

'Oh, Jane. It's gorgeous.'

'I know.'

'Here. Let me help you put it on.'

Jane was pleased with the help because when she tried to undo the zipper she was surprised to find her hand trembling. She didn't even have time to think about the scars on her body or that Louise might see them. She was far too excited to be self-conscious. When the dress was on, Jane stared at herself in the mirror, gobsmacked at her reflection.

'I look…beautiful.' She spoke the word as though she'd never thought of herself in that way before.

Louise laughed. 'Of course you do, darling.' She pointed to Jane's feet. 'You need shoes and, do you know, I think I have just the pair. Good thing we're the same size. Be right back.'

Jane turned one way then the other, unable to believe it was really her in the reflection. She looked at her hair and held it up from her neck, bunching the long locks, trying to figure out what sort of style suited the dress. Finally, she pulled half of it back, leaving the rest hanging loose down her back. 'That works.'

Louise returned a moment later with the shoes and also a small necklace which was made from diamonds and sapphires in the shape of little daisies. 'Look what else I found. It was Sean's grandmother's.'

'Blue daisies,' Jane gasped, and when Louise clasped the necklace around her neck, Jane couldn't believe how perfectly it all fitted. Even the borrowed shoes matched.

'I like what you've done with your hair,' Louise said. 'Perfect. Now, how about a little bit of make-up? Just a touch of blush and a bit of lip gloss?'

Jane nodded deciding that as tonight was going to be her very special pre-birthday dinner with Sean, and he'd gone to such trouble to buy her the dress, she wanted to be the perfect princess for her very own prince.

When Louise had finished applying the make-up, giggling that she felt very much like the fairy godmother getting Cinderella ready for the ball, Jane slipped her glasses back on and stared at her reflection in stunned disbelief.

'Oh, my. I really *am* a princess.'

Louise laughed. 'I can't wait for Sean to see you.'

'Me neither.' Jane smoothed her hand down the dress.

'Well, go on, then,' Louise prompted, pointing to the door. 'I'm sure your chariot awaits.'

Jane laughed and headed for the door, walking with more pride and self-assurance than she could ever remember feeling before. It was Sean. He had come into her life, enhancing it beyond measure.

As she descended the stairs, it wasn't Sean but Spencer, who was dressed for bed, who saw her first.

'Mummy!' he gasped, unable to stop himself from staring at her.

The word made Jane's moment even more complete.

'You're so beautiful,' he breathed.

'That's an understatement, son,' Sean remarked, walking over to take Jane's hand in his, bringing it to his lips and kissing it in a gallant gesture. 'Stunning.'

She smiled shyly. 'Thank you for the dress. It's…the prettiest thing I've ever worn.'

Sean seemed genuinely choked up at the sight of her and simply nodded, acknowledging her words.

'You two had better get going,' Louise interjected a moment later as the two of them just stood there, staring into each other's eyes.

'Yes.' Sean was the first to snap out of it. 'Let's say goodnight to Spencer.'

Jane bent down and held out her arms to Spencer, who immediately ran to her. He wrapped his arms about her neck and kissed her cheek. 'I can't wait until you're my real mummy. It's so exciting,' he squeaked, before his father scooped him up and blew a raspberry on his tummy, peals of delighted laughter filling the air.

'Don't razz him up too much,' Louise complained, glaring pointedly at her son.

'True. True.' With that, Sean pressed one last kiss to

his son's cheek and put him back on the floor. 'Brush your teeth and remember to do exactly what Grandma says, OK?'

'Yes, Dad.' Spencer rolled his eyes as though he'd already been through this drill.

'Right, then.' Sean crooked his arm towards Jane who immediately placed her hand around his elbow. 'Shall we?'

'We shall,' she returned, and it wasn't until she was walking out the door that Louise gave her a small fabric bag, which she slipped over Jane's wrist.

'Has a bit of lippy in it in case you need a touch-up later on.'

'Oh. Thanks.'

'Happy birthday.' Louise and Spencer waved, Barney coming to join them as they all waved the birthday girl off on her adventure.

The instant Sean had reversed out of the driveway, Louise turned to her husband and grandson. 'Action stations!' she declared, and they all quickly set about putting the rest of the night's events into motion.

It wasn't until after dinner, eaten by candlelight in a secluded gourmet restaurant, that Jane looked across the table at Sean and realised that something was going on.

'Is that your phone buzzing again?'

'Yes.'

'I hope it's not an emergency, although if it is, we'll deal with it.'

'It's not the hospital,' he replied.

'Oh.' Anxiety marred her features as she watched him read the text message. 'Is it Spencer?'

'No, no.' Sean smiled at her. 'Everything is fine...except for the little surprise I have for you.' He motioned to the waiter and a moment later a box wrapped in pretty

birthday paper with daisies all over it was placed in front
of her. 'Happy birthday, Jane.'

'A present? I thought the dinner was my present.'

'Open it,' he encouraged, watching her closely.

'OK.' Jane smiled as she ran her hands over the box
that looked as though it contained a bottle of wine. Carefully she peeled off the paper, pleased when Sean didn't
try to rush her. Finally, she removed the paper and looked
at what was inside. 'Cinnamon!'

'No one's going to wreck this doll,' Sean said softly.
'Her hair is almost as long as yours but I have to say yours
is much more impressive, and silky and soft and...' He
breathed out, repressed desire in his eyes. 'And you know
I want to run my fingers through it right now.'

Jane held his gaze and nodded, the doll still firmly in
her hands. 'Then we'd better get out of here,' she suggested, and he nodded. 'I can't believe you remembered
the doll. This is the most perfect present, Sean. Thank you.'

He stood from his seat and came around to hold her
chair, and she instantly pressed her lips to his. 'Thank
you,' she said again.

'You're more than welcome,' he remarked, letting his
hands trail slowly through her free-flowing locks.

Jane sighed. 'I guess it is almost pumpkin time.'

'Pumpkin time?'

She smiled at him as they said goodbye to the proprietor. 'Midnight,' she tut-tutted as they walked to his car.
'You have two sisters who no doubt dressed up as fairy-
tale princesses when they were younger and yet you have
no idea what "pumpkin time" means?'

He shrugged. 'My sisters were always a puzzle to me
when we were growing up.' He held the car door for her,
pressing a kiss to her lips before quickly going around to

the driver's side. Even there, he seemed a little preoccupied and almost…nervous.

'Sean? Is everything all right?'

'Of course it is. Why wouldn't it be?' he said as he drove them away from the city, towards Port Adelaide. 'I just have one more little surprise for your birthday and then we can think about heading home.'

'OK,' she said, her nerves settling with his reassuring tone. She dug around in the little handbag Louise had given her and reapplied the lip gloss, before closing her eyes and allowing herself to listen to the soothing classical music Sean had switched on.

'I'm having such a wonderful time,' she said dreamily, her words relaxed and floating away on the breeze. 'I can't believe how much I love you, Sean. How much you mean to me. I never want to let you go. I never want to be apart from you. You've made my world.'

'That's good to hear,' he said as he slowed the car and finally brought it to a stop. It was only then she realised he'd parked the car and that they were at the port. Outside her window was a small cruising yacht, covered in fairy-lights.

'Wow. Will you look at that? It's gorgeous.'

Sean came around the car to help her out before pulling her close and dropping another kiss to her lips. 'Happy prebirthday surprise,' he whispered, gesturing to the yacht.

'Huh?' But it was only as her eyes adjusted to the light that she was able to see the people who were already on board the yacht. Louise was there with Barney and Spencer, Sean's sisters and their families, as well as Luc, Anthea, Romana and a score of their other friends from the hospital.

'Sean?'

LUCY CLARK 183

'Happy surprise wedding,' he said, then took her hand and led her towards the gangplank. 'It's all organised.'

Jane gasped. 'The dress.'

'Something new,' he commented.

Jane touched the blue sapphire necklace at her throat. 'And this?'

'Something old and something blue.'

A giggle worked its way up as she looked down at the shoes. 'And, of course, my something borrowed.' She nodded in appreciation. 'Very clever,' she said as she allowed him to escort her onto the yacht, where they were greeted by a round of welcoming applause.

'I think my mother deserves an award for her performance,' Sean said.

'And Spencer. How did he keep this a secret?'

'He nearly didn't. Not when he saw you looking so beautiful,' he replied as he continued to lead her through the parting crowd towards the bow, where a marriage celebrant stood waiting for them. 'As difficult as it's been to keep the secret, wanting to share so much of it with you, your reaction, your appreciation, your trust in allowing me to do all of this for you, to give you the most perfect night of your life, has been wonderful.'

'No. Not wonderful, Dad. *Purple*,' Spencer interjected, rolling his eyes.

They both laughed. 'It *is* purple, Sean.' She grinned as she said the words. 'The most perfect purple and green night of all time.'

They stopped before the marriage celebrant and she turned to face Sean, holding his hands tightly in hers, doing her best not to cry from overwhelming happiness.

'Dearly beloved,' the celebrant began, but Jane couldn't contain her love for Sean any more and stood on tiptoe and kissed him passionately, in front of everyone.

'I haven't got to that part yet,' the celebrant murmured, but neither Sean nor Jane cared. Against all odds, they'd found each other, bonded together in a love that would last a lifetime.

* * * * *

Mills & Boon® Hardback
April 2014

ROMANCE

A D'Angelo Like No Other	Carole Mortimer
Seduced by the Sultan	Sharon Kendrick
When Christakos Meets His Match	Abby Green
The Purest of Diamonds?	Susan Stephens
Secrets of a Bollywood Marriage	Susanna Carr
What the Greek's Money Can't Buy	Maya Blake
The Last Prince of Dahaar	Tara Pammi
The Sicilian's Unexpected Duty	Michelle Smart
One Night with Her Ex	Lucy King
The Secret Ingredient	Nina Harrington
Her Soldier Protector	Soraya Lane
Stolen Kiss From a Prince	Teresa Carpenter
Behind the Film Star's Smile	Kate Hardy
The Return of Mrs Jones	Jessica Gilmore
Her Client from Hell	Louisa George
Flirting with the Forbidden	Joss Wood
The Last Temptation of Dr Dalton	Robin Gianna
Resisting Her Rebel Hero	Lucy Ryder

MEDICAL

200 Harley Street: Surgeon in a Tux	Carol Marinelli
200 Harley Street: Girl from the Red Carpet	Scarlet Wilson
Flirting with the Socialite Doc	Melanie Milburne
His Diamond Like No Other	Lucy Clark

0314GEN STD HB

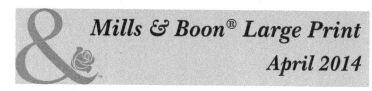

Mills & Boon® Large Print
April 2014

ROMANCE

Defiant in the Desert — Sharon Kendrick
Not Just the Boss's Plaything — Caitlin Crews
Rumours on the Red Carpet — Carole Mortimer
The Change in Di Navarra's Plan — Lynn Raye Harris
The Prince She Never Knew — Kate Hewitt
His Ultimate Prize — Maya Blake
More than a Convenient Marriage? — Dani Collins
Second Chance with Her Soldier — Barbara Hannay
Snowed in with the Billionaire — Caroline Anderson
Christmas at the Castle — Marion Lennox
Beware of the Boss — Leah Ashton

HISTORICAL

Not Just a Wallflower — Carole Mortimer
Courted by the Captain — Anne Herries
Running from Scandal — Amanda McCabe
The Knight's Fugitive Lady — Meriel Fuller
Falling for the Highland Rogue — Ann Lethbridge

MEDICAL

Gold Coast Angels: A Doctor's Redemption — Marion Lennox
Gold Coast Angels: Two Tiny Heartbeats — Fiona McArthur
Christmas Magic in Heatherdale — Abigail Gordon
The Motherhood Mix-Up — Jennifer Taylor
The Secret Between Them — Lucy Clark
Craving Her Rough Diamond Doc — Amalie Berlin

Mills & Boon® Hardback

May 2014

ROMANCE

The Only Woman to Defy Him	Carol Marinelli
Secrets of a Ruthless Tycoon	Cathy Williams
Gambling with the Crown	Lynn Raye Harris
The Forbidden Touch of Sanguardo	Julia James
One Night to Risk it All	Maisey Yates
A Clash with Cannavaro	Elizabeth Power
The Truth About De Campo	Jennifer Hayward
Sheikh's Scandal	Lucy Monroe
Beach Bar Baby	Heidi Rice
Sex, Lies & Her Impossible Boss	Jennifer Rae
Lessons in Rule-Breaking	Christy McKellen
Twelve Hours of Temptation	Shoma Narayanan
Expecting the Prince's Baby	Rebecca Winters
The Millionaire's Homecoming	Cara Colter
The Heir of the Castle	Scarlet Wilson
Swept Away by the Tycoon	Barbara Wallace
Return of Dr Maguire	Judy Campbell
Heatherdale's Shy Nurse	Abigail Gordon

MEDICAL

200 Harley Street: The Proud Italian	Alison Roberts
200 Harley Street: American Surgeon in London	Lynne Marshall
A Mother's Secret	Scarlet Wilson
Saving His Little Miracle	Jennifer Taylor

Mills & Boon® Large Print
May 2014

ROMANCE

The Dimitrakos Proposition	Lynne Graham
His Temporary Mistress	Cathy Williams
A Man Without Mercy	Miranda Lee
The Flaw in His Diamond	Susan Stephens
Forged in the Desert Heat	Maisey Yates
The Tycoon's Delicious Distraction	Maggie Cox
A Deal with Benefits	Susanna Carr
Mr (Not Quite) Perfect	Jessica Hart
English Girl in New York	Scarlet Wilson
The Greek's Tiny Miracle	Rebecca Winters
The Final Falcon Says I Do	Lucy Gordon

HISTORICAL

From Ruin to Riches	Louise Allen
Protected by the Major	Anne Herries
Secrets of a Gentleman Escort	Bronwyn Scott
Unveiling Lady Clare	Carol Townend
A Marriage of Notoriety	Diane Gaston

MEDICAL

Gold Coast Angels: Bundle of Trouble	Fiona Lowe
Gold Coast Angels: How to Resist Temptation	Amy Andrews
Her Firefighter Under the Mistletoe	Scarlet Wilson
Snowbound with Dr Delectable	Susan Carlisle
Her Real Family Christmas	Kate Hardy
Christmas Eve Delivery	Connie Cox

Discover more romance at

www.millsandboon.co.uk

- ❤ WIN great prizes in our exclusive competitions
- ❤ BUY new titles before they hit the shops
- ❤ BROWSE new books and REVIEW your favourites
- ❤ SAVE on new books with the Mills & Boon® Bookclub™
- ❤ DISCOVER new authors

PLUS, to chat about your favourite reads, get the latest news and find special offers:

- 📘 Find us on facebook.com/millsandboon
- 🐦 Follow us on twitter.com/millsandboonuk
- ❤ Sign up to our newsletter at millsandboon.co.uk